# "Adventure Travel" in Guatemala

## The Maya Heritage

## Mark J. Curran

 **www.trafford.com**
**North America & international**
toll-free: 844-688-6899 (USA & Canada)
fax: 812 355 4082

# AUTHOR'S DISCLAIMER

*I'm writing this book in 2021 and 2022, but the story I'm telling is fiction, combining history, art, architecture, and tourism, and takes place in 1980. My own travels to Guatemala were first in 1962, then again in 1969 and 1970 for very short visits, and extensively with my wife Keah in 1976 and 1977. I must tell the reader that I was uninformed of the real situation, especially in those latter years. To the tourist, the country was still beautiful. There are no excuses for me. The color remained, Guatemala's famous indigenous Maya villages, small farming, and weaving.*

*In 1962 I was on the buses, first in Mexico after classes at the UNAM, then to the Guatemala border and then on down to Quetzaltenango, all in a very folkloric trip. In that visit I experienced what amounts to a very sheltered view of Guatemala through an upper-class college friend from school days in Kansas City, Missouri from 1959 to 1962. The country seemed wonderful, a paradise of nature and with the vestiges of the Spanish Colonial Heritage and the modern views of the descendants of the Maya in their syncretic religious ceremonies, the "cofradia" or religious brotherhood in the church in Chichicastenango, the villages around Lake Atitlán and of course in Antigua. I fell in love with the country. I was even offered a job to stay, but graduate school was the goal.*

*The visit in 1969 and again in 1970 were the same, a whirlwind of tourism after Brazil.*

*I directed the Arizona State University Summer Program at the Universidad Francisco Marroquín (they called it "The Harvard of Central America") in 1976 and 1977, accompanied by my wife Keah both times, in 1977 she well along in her pregnancy.*

*Each year we had about twenty – five students housed in "pensiones," and we all did the standard tourist forays on the weekends. (I think today it was a miracle that no disasters befell us.) The big change in Guatemala was the aftermath of the horrendous earthquake of early 1976. We at A.S.U. were seriously considering cancelling the summer program prior to June of that year but were assured that "things were better". We saw the devastation of the "better." But we also witnessed that "off to the side" business mentioned earlier: poverty was evident everywhere including the shanty towns down the hill from Guatemala City's downtown and National Palace and evident in the countryside when we passed through villages and hiked at Atitlán.*

*We of course noted the guards at the National Palace with submachine guns (standard practice in such places as Peru or Brazil where I had spent time) and occasional military trucks or small convoys armed to the teeth at various places, but the color was still there, the Maya ladies with their weavings, the battered remains of churches in Antigua, Guatemala City, and the highlands. Someone did point out to us the bullet holes in the walls of buildings in Sololá on the way to Lake Atitlán, but no one, and I mean no one, including that spiffy faculty at the University talked of the "Guatemala Solution" to the supposed threat of Ché, Fidel and the Left in the Country. I did have an inkling of the bandied about phrase – "Land Reform," - but only in bits and pieces. It turns out to all be very complicated, and so much was not revealed in the international press until the 1990s from firsthand witnesses like Rigoberta Menchu. And I hesitate to say, the role of United States' politics, military "aid" and intervention to in effect make Guatemala an armed, military state.*

*I do not pretend to delve into Guatemala's "Dirty War" which lasted thirty some years. Suffice to say it is yet another of the great human tragedies of our times. I today have enough experience to know that most on both sides sincerely believed in their version of the reality. I have been chagrinned and saddened by what I have learned, and today's mass migration north is therefore no surprise. I am not here to write a condemnation nor even a description of those days and years.*

*Much of this book will be the re - creation of my memories of pleasant times (not all, most) and what this small country idealistically could offer when at its best. I have had* to do the same with writings in fiction of Brazil. I do not intend to ignore the ugly reality but strive to create a read that basically expresses my mindset before I found out the "other side." I'm just starting, so let's see how it goes, how it evolves. My only defense: I loved what I saw of the country and its people.

# PROLOGUE

The reader (hopefully a few more than that) may recall the book combining culture and fiction, "Portugal and Spain on the 'International Adventurer'" of 1977. It recounted the trip and adventures of Mike Gaherty and uh, … colleague, friend, sometime lover, ex – fiancée, Amy Carrier in Portugal and Spain of that year. All was successful, albeit with some surprises, and we made it home, but now we are "just friends." Amy was the one who is responsible for that decision. Okay.

It all ended in the "post – trip" meeting with Adventure Travel's CEO James Morrison in the office in Los Angeles. He had great praise for our work in Portugal and Spain and an amazing commendation from no less than veteran Harry Downing (he of more than one hundred AT trips) for both Amy and me. James at that "decompression" meeting expressed a desire for us to continue with projects and trips, the one "on the table" would be an AT trip to Guatemala, with a side trip to Copán in Honduras. A significant part of that choice was my extensive research, travel, and teaching respective of that area highlighting both the colonial charm of Guatemala but especially the Indigenous heritage today and the outstanding Pre – Columbian sites like Tikal and Copán. In fact, I had done a preliminary outline adding Guatemala to our original Mexico trip, but it turned out, wisely, that it was just too much for one trip. Hence the "tabled" notion. James had kept the original itinerary plan in his files, so there was nothing new, I mean, nothing to sell him on.

Time has passed; it is now 1980 and I'm still a happy Professor of Spanish and Portuguese at the University of Nebraska in Lincoln, teaching those languages plus respective cultures both of the Peninsula and the Americas. It goes well with significant research completed on Brazil, and publications, hence the boost to the rank of Associate Professor (with a freeze on the promotion dollars but that small raise came a year later).

Amy has continued with her full-time dedication to AT and trip planning the past three years. We are in touch but there are no romantic developments to report. Me, I'm lonely, not finding anyone serious in Lincoln although there has been a lot of dating of one or two of the Department of Languages and Literatures colleagues. So, it remains to be seen what may be in store for Amy and me. She did get enthusiastic about a reunion on the research trip to Guatemala, reiterating we had enjoyed some wonderful times together but re – reiterating she liked just being good friends. I'll take that for now. We met in Los Angeles in April and set up the plan for our investigating the layout for a possible AT trip for the summer of 1981.

The reader may also have seen my book on our joint research for AT in Mexico in 1974, "Pre – Columbian Mexico. Plans, Pitfalls and Perils." I won't spoil it for a new reader or two due to mentioning it now; just buy the rare book (in terms of sales) if you want to know the whole story (the same message my "literatura de cordel" poets in Brazil tell the public when they recite only part of their story – poems in the marketplace or fairs). What you do need to know is that good ole' Mexico provided incredible travel adventures but also Amy and I almost lost our lives trying to complete the research. One word – Xolotl. That did bond us together.

Amy wanted to know right away if the upcoming project would be dangerous like Mexico, "If that is the case, count me out!" I assured her I could not ever believe that the Mexico perils would be repeated and just expected a fun trip, some travel adventure to be sure, but no more than that. And I expressed my joy at, well, just us being together again. We would be sharing accommodations and be together for about three weeks, close company one imagines. Amy seems fine with that so she began her usual competent work for travel, hotels, restaurants, and all, making decisions on all that for the AT travelers for the trip, ahem, should it all work out.

Here's the original plan as approved by James Morrison (but subject to change) with the usual agreement on salary, expenses and the like, travelers' checks, and the AT credit card. Amy always had passports and such up to date, but we both had to obtain the tourist cards for Guatemala and Honduras, all to be done prior to June. It would be the rainy season, but I reasoned we wanted to see a "green" Guatemala and not the browns of the winter dry season. That meant tropical downpours at times, muddy roads, but worth the discomfort in my view. After all, it was I who was on the hook for what we would see.

History and Travel in the Maya World - Guatemala and Honduras

| | |
|---|---|
| Day 1. | Flight to Guatemala City – Hotel |
| Day 2. | Kaminaljuyu – Olmec - Maya – Teotihuacano early site. National Palace. Archeological Museum |
| Day 3. | Van to Antigua. Ciudad Vieja, Antigua - Plaza, Conventos, Shopping |
| Day 4. | San Antonio Águas Calientes. Indigenous town and weaving, Iglesia de San Francisco, Iglesia de Santo Domingo |
| Day 5. | Van to El Lago de Atitlán, Mail Boat to Santiago Atitlán |
| Day 6. | Hike around the Lake, fishing, free time, Casa Contenta Dinner |
| Day 7. | Mercado de Chichicastenango, Church of Santo Domingo and the religious syncretism of the shamen and the "Cofradía." |
| Day 8. | Van to Guatemala City, Flight to Tikal |
| Day 9, 10. | Tikal, Archeological Site, Museum, Hike in Forest. Exploration |
| Day 11. | Return to Guatemala City |
| Day 12. | Van to town of Copán Ruinas, Honduras |
| Day 13. | Copán Ruínas |
| Day 14. | Return to Guatemala City. Flight Home |

# 1

## IN THE AIR TO GUATEMALA CITY

In early June we had met in Denver and spent a night at Amy's parents' home where I was reintroduced to her parents. I do not know exactly how she explained to them the end of our engagement in late summer of 1977 after the AT trip to Portugal and Spain, but there were no questions, just a warm welcome to "Amy's old friend." They did say they were pleased that I had added to her myriad adventures on the planet with the trips to Brazil, Mexico, and the Spanish- Portuguese Peninsula. We did not discuss Xolotl and Mexico, and I'm not sure Amy ever mentioned him to them. Just as well. We talked some of time since then, Amy on the ships, me teaching at Nebraska, but there were no uneasy moments.

The next morning, we took off on Aviateca from the huge Denver airport, documents and plans in hand, luggage for the three – week stay. The reader knows the object of our trip: research and scoping out the area for the Hispanic Heritage, modern colorful Indigenous scenes and mainly once again the Pre – Columbian Maya sites. I'm sure there are many anecdotes I'll recall from my past trips there, but as they come up. It would be, we hoped, like old times with Amy in charge of selecting the best of hotels and restaurants, me just hoping my stomach would hold up with the local delicacies. The flight provided a good airline meal, a scotch for me and wine for Amy, and just enough time to go over the tentative itinerary.

I've always thought that Guatemala was one of the most beautiful places I had ever seen, perhaps a romanticized view from past trips, more to recall as we go along, but the arrival shortly after noon was impressive, the plane circling the huge valley the city is nestled in, all green, and with those volcanoes, one active, circling the area. We were met by our Adventure Travel (from now on AT) driver Rodolfo, but I noticed in passing it was an unmarked van (we would talk about that later), whisked through customs, and driven to the Hilton through busy streets jammed with cars, buses, and smoke belching trucks. He would be our man for most of the travel in coming days and weeks.

We were booked by Amy at the very upscale Hilton in Guatemala City, "sold" to me when I found out it was near the "Nuestra Señora de los Remedios" church, memorable from trips past and my own introduction to Guatemala way back in the 60s as a student and visiting my friend Val Meier from Creighton undergraduate days in Omaha. It is not yet planned, but I'm sure I can convince Amy to make that uniquely beautiful small church a priority in tourism in the city. Rodolfo was friendly, gracious, and his Spanish was clear with that "voseo" used by the upper-class locals, "Qué tal vós?" I wondered where the second person familiar "tú" I had learned in Spanish in the United States had gone.

He was assigned as well as an informant by AT in Guatemala and we learned he had a degree in History from the national university. He joked, "What can you do with a history degree? I should have studied business or law. Ha ha. But I can tell you between studies and now work for years for AT, I know all the ins and outs of Guatemala, and I'm here to make your visit an informed visit."

I said, "Great! What I personally think (and I believe Amy will agree with me) is that we be given the complete story wherever we are; there can be no surprises for us or for possible Adventurers. I'm thinking a 'pro' and 'con' summary. Que tal?"

"Naturalmente! Sin duda esto puedo hacer y con mucho gusto. Solo que sepan que no siempre estará agradable la descripción. De acuerdo?" ["Naturally. Without doubt I can do that, and with great pleasure. Only that you know that the description will not always be pleasant. Agreed?"] We both agreed.

Back to that first day. We would eat a late lunch at the hotel, organize a bit and Rodolfo would come by at 3:00 for a late afternoon introduction to the city. He thought the old historic center downtown would be a good choice – the National Palace, the National Cathedral, and plazas. I don't know the name of it, but there is a "mid – town" much more modern, with small sky – scrapers and mainly the business part of town. I had a chance to ask Rodolfo why the unmarked van, no AT logo or such. His answer was a bit revealing.

"Miguel and Amy, Guatemala is safe for tourists and researchers just like you now in 1980 mainly because the military and right – wing conservative politicians have an iron grip on the country. Most of the violence has been in the countryside with a beefed-up military, incidentally, supported with heavy arms, helicopters, and such from your country, hunting down leftists and often with a 'shoot on sight' anyone they think may have abetted the Left. That includes a lot of Indigenous people supposedly supplying then with shelter and food. Ha! As if Indians have extra food! What you will see is a result of this 'Pax Militar,' people with their heads down and their mouths shut and living as best they can in the present. No tourists have been targeted, and most of what you and AT are interested in remains intact. The van has no logo because simply anything North American like 'Adventure Travel' could be seen as 'yanqui,' and it's best to play it safe."

Amy reacted more strongly than me, but I felt it. She said, "Here we go again Gaherty, but this seems a hell of a lot more dangerous than a few Indian nationalists in Mexico. You said, and I don't know who else said, things were 'better' here. Honestly, I'm scared to death and at the first sign of any danger to us or to our potential 'Adventurers' I will call it all off."

Rodolfo quickly retorted, "Amy, I understand, believe me, but there is next to zero danger to tourists. Guatemala needs them and their money, and their/ your safety is a priority. If I had not told you this, you would have never suspected anything! Our country is presenting its best face to you. I think your fears will be assuaged tomorrow when I take you to meet Nataniel Schmidt the agent for AT here in Guatemala City. Please be assured I am telling you the truth. My only aim was to give you a bit of background and explain the current situation."

I took Amy's hand, squeezed it trying to calm her and said, "I'm with Rodolfo, and I'm not worried. Let's make the best of it." She gave me that fiery look I had seen before, still shook her head, but said, "Okay. But don't expect me to be at my best with lots of laughs and jokes. De ninguna manera! ["No way!"]."

Rodolfo took us on to the main plaza in front of the National Palace and said, "You will enjoy this amazing place; it puts that old grey, stone national palace in Mexico City to shame. (Disclaimer by this author: that is, except for Diego Rivera's famous mural "Historia de México.") Guatemala in many ways is just a 'small Mexico' but one ups it in surprising ways." I suppose so.

## THE PALACE

It had to be on the priority list for any Adventurers as we would see. Finished by President General (Dictator) Jorge Úbico in 1939, it did dazzle. We were greeted by those guards with sub-machine guns, incidentally of indigenous ethnicity. The problem was the palace was done with prisoner – slave labor at 25 cents per day, but then no one objected. Some call it the "Guacalomón" [The Big Guacamole] due to the greenish colored brick exterior, Úbico's supposedly favorite color. I'm glad there is some vestige of humor about the man and the place. I suspect the nickname came after his demise.

Here are some scenes we saw, and incidentally it was all "tourism," no hassles from those guards. They did inspect our hand luggage and, pardon me, ogled Amy. We thought they were teenagers, probably enlisted as it were.

Amy and I concluded that the Presidential Palace really was little different from other palaces in many respects, including some Neo – Classic buildings in the United States built with slave labor, and, yes, a plenitude of gold.

There was a bit of a letdown when we wandered the grounds in front of the palace, a rather scruffy Minerva Park, and if one walked to one edge, a "barranca" or canyon filled with ramshackle huts of tin and scrap lumber, "homes" we were told of the victims of the earthquake of 1976. We would see more. Oh, and I forgot, one scene that was fascinating, but kitsch in appearance, the cement 3D relief map of Guatemala in the park. Well – worn, in need of a new paint job, but positive in one sense: one really got a feeling for this land of forests, mountains and volcanoes! (I could only remember all the same from the bus ride into Guatemala from La Mesilla - El Tapón on the border with Mexico after school at the UNAM in 1962 in Mexico City (my Guatemalan friend's father was amazed I was on that road in a school-bus). That harrowing ride was followed by the highlands of western Guatemala at Quetzaltenango and later the entrance at night into the city with friend Val and the "Volcán de Fuego" spewing fire and lava in all its glory. In need of a paint job, now aging gracefully since 1905, you have an idea from the map, a small park in itself, of the diversity of the country's terrain, of the no less than 37 volcanoes (my college friend's brother had as a goal – hobby to climb them all) and the coastal plains east and west. Guatemala by the way is an Indian word meaning "place of many trees." It was and still is up to a point; I'll talk about the harvesting of rare hardwoods in the Petén region later.

There was time after the Palace to meet AT's agent in Guatemala, Señor Nataniel Schmidt, in his very comfortable office in business mid – town, near the Guatemalan Tourist Commission. Nataniel had been apprised by AT CEO James Morrison in Los Angeles that we would be coming to his country, and he knew of our project and plans. He greeted us warmly, a handshake to me and light embrace to Amy (all with protocol, but she said later she had seen that look before). Amy told me later she had this "déjà vu" memory of greetings by AT's man in Mexico City and subsequent events! Okay, down to business! Nataniel knew our plan and repeated much of Rodolfo's spiel – "Yes, all is safe with tourism as long as you are careful, but he can take care of any surprises should they come up" (Amy looked daggers at me again). We went over the itinerary, checking off places, and he really had nothing to add, gave us his portable phone number and wished us well. We would do a full day in the city tomorrow before the jaunt to Antigua. We, ahem, did not talk politics.

Amy found a high-end restaurant for our first fine dining experience; readers know from past books that I would just say "Yes ma'am; we are on your turf." We had a wonderful dinner that evening at, you guessed, Jean Francois's place. Positive points are the location and style, advertised to be like "A hacienda in Antigua," with many patios, lush vegetation, and a menu to match. The featured beef dish was my choice, she had seafood in some kind of fancy French sauce (what else?), and we enjoyed not one but two bottles of wine. You could see Volcán de Fuego in the distance. But for me, as good as the food was, it was once again hearing a fine marimba band which took me back to earlier days at Lake Atitlán at the Casa Contenta in 1962. It was that occasion I was introduced by friend Val to beautiful upper class Guatemalan young ladies and danced with them, albeit not well, to marimba music. Of shall we say lesser importance; that was when the young Nebraska farm boy was introduced to scotch by Eduardo's brothers and uncle. It was Johnny Walker Red, and I did not like it much, … at first. I mentioned only part of that evening to Amy, the part about the marimba music.

"I loved that music from twenty years ago and have a well-played 33 RPM record at home I still put on once in a while. Amy, there is nothing quite like it. The musicians are always indigenous fellows in full Maya regalia, the beautiful woven shirts, and even embroidered trousers." We danced a bit to beautiful tunes after dinner. Always associated with the Maya with a long history including the recent repression, and at times schmaltzy and for show (this was not the case at our restaurant), some say the marimba is like a xylophone but all I can say is it is made from various woods, played with wooden mallets and makes me happy. Or was it the wine?

A small thing perhaps, but Monsieur Françoise had beautiful reproductions of paintings of Frida Kahlo in our dining room, not very 'Teco' to be sure, but with our good memories of study of her on the Mexico trip. The crowd by the way was strictly upper – class, coat and tie and evening dress (Amy was forewarned, so we dressed accordingly), and with many foreigners. Okay. We would begin to see the "real" Guatemala in a day or two. I did not see the bill, which was handled by Amy, but she even gulped a bit, "There goes a chunk of James Morrison's budget for us. But AT travelers cannot miss this!"

Back in our hotel room we made a plan for the next day, slept well due to being exhausted from the flight and the day. The next morning it was time to delve into local spots in the city related to the Mayas. First was a visit to Kaminaljuhu and then the Archeological Museum. The first was an ancient dig of Pre – Classic times when the early Maya were in touch with the vast site of Teotihuacán in Mexico, circa 250 A.D. (it turns out Teotihuacán exercised influence even at Tikal, to be seen). Construction was adobe so little was left, and honestly, not too impressive, yet important historically. We both decided it would be of interest only to the fans among the Adventurers with archeological interests.

Much more impressive was the small but quality Archeological Museum nearby, including some fine examples of that Maya forté - the Stelae. I took photos but neglected to title them, suffice to say they were from the later Classic Period of high Maya culture, 300 to 900 A.D. It did whet our appetites for what we knew was coming, Tikal in Guatemala and Copán in Honduras.

The archeological mockup of Tikal was indeed impressive, to be seen. I was salivating at actually seeing that major Maya site.

After lunch, we did, well, the churches. Once again, we are a bit out of order chronologically since Guatemala City as capital only came into existence in the late 17th century after the capital was moved from Almolonga and Antigua of the 16th century. There was still massive damage visible from the earthquake of 1976, and honestly it was sad. We both thought that Adventurers would want to see the old Cathedral perhaps more from witnessing just what an earthquake could do. One jewel however was Nuestra Señora de las Angustias, a "privately" financed and constructed church I had marveled at in past years with friend Val, attending mass there with his family. Its doors and altar pieces of wonderful carved wood.

The next day would be one of jewels of Guatemala – Antigua.

# 2

## ON THE WAY TO AND IN ANTIGUA

Because of recent flooding (is there never enough natural disaster in Guatemala?), we had to take the Pan American Highway north and northwest to the intersection before Chilpancingo and then back down south to Antigua, but it would not be a long ride and, besides, would take us through green, beautiful countryside. That was when we experienced our first encounter with the modern Maya on this trip. We saw just off the highway a large, open, tin roofed building but with many Maya ladies and children and with all kinds of clothing laying on the grassy hillside drying in the sun. Rodolfo explained that it is a community "pila" or water faucet and tanks to wash clothes, ostensibly for the indigenous small town nearby. I said, "Pictures?" Rodolfo smiled and said, "Sure."

I had learned years before that the indigenous people refrain from allowing tourists to take personal photos of them, the reason, an old belief that a photo can "capture" the spirit or soul of a person. But on this trip, there would many exceptions, Rodolfo explaining that a small "present" or "offering" would seldom be refused, they just needed the cash too badly. We carefully sidled up to a Maya mother, her two young daughters perhaps 8 and 10 years of age to her side, all in traditional woven Maya "huipiles" [blouses] and skirts. The mother was washing articles of clothing with a bar of soap on the slanted "washboard" stone surface of the "pila" but looked up and smiled as we approached. I could assume she was used to tourists with cameras but asked in Spanish if we could take a picture and I had a small "present" to her for the "privilegio" [privilege]. I took the photo but, in my nervousness, must have moved the camera. I would only know that later when the slide was developed.

We had a short conversation, discovering her name was (what else in the current Catholic world) María and the daughters Juanita and Socorro, her husband Pedro was away, doing seasonal work down near the Pacific coast cutting sugar cane for a big hacienda. We would discover this was perhaps the only way most of the Maya families could make it, seasonal work for very low wages, but a few "quetzales" (the Guatemalan currency, curiously enough valued one on one with the dollar). Since there was no running water in anybody's house, this was the nearest place to wash clothes (2 kilometers distant). I asked about drinking water and María said there was one spigot for all families in the central plaza of her small town. I would guess her age at about 40 but she looked older and, well, tired. Amy explained in Spanish we were traveling to her beautiful country to do research for planning a trip for the next year and were in fact just beginning and on our way to Antigua.

"I know it well; several of us ladies and the kids go there every weekend on the bus and sell weavings and toys we make at home. We need every bit of income to make it."

On an impulse (the reader of any past books knows I am indeed impulsive) that provided an opening. "María, if we were to come to your house and look at your weavings it would be our pleasure to make a purchase or two. If you gather your washing, we can all get in the van, go to your place, and do this." Socorro spoke in a rather painful voice to her mother, in a Maya dialect. All I got was "No, mamita," and then in what Rodolfo told me was a dialect of k'iché (he knows some words but admitted he was nowhere fluent). María then looked at us, almost in tears and said in halting Spanish, "My daughter is upset. She is ashamed for anyone to see our house, where we live. Señor, we are very poor, but I really need any money we can bring in, so what to do?"

I said, "Señora, first of all, we will totally respect your wishes; if you want, we can wait outside on the street or even at the van wherever we park, but I would like to tell you we both have visited very poor areas of Brazil and Peru and Mexico. We mean no discomfort to you." María seemed relieved, "Perhaps waiting at the van." We helped her gather three large plastic baskets, I guess each of them would carry one, María the largest, put them all in the back of the van and piled in. I insisted María sit in the right passenger seat and Amy and I would go in the seats to the rear with the girls.

María gave halting instructions in broken Spanish, but it took about fifteen minutes on an incredibly rough dirt country road filled with rocks to reach her village of Finca La Colona. The sight was at first sobering, a tiny village of perhaps four streets, only one cobblestoned, the rest hard clay, very poor - looking row houses of adobe mud brick and tin roofs, most with wooden windows and doors. There was a tiny plaza, and I noted the stone, round "pila" with a single faucet, several Maya women surrounding it, each with large plastic jars (we were told the old clay jars were replaced years ago because the plastic was so much lighter, and incidentally, did not break if you dropped it). There were Maya men at each entrance to each street with large clubs in their hands; they wore what looked like a local version of cowboy hat, black woven jackets and white pants. We parked across the street from the houses, María got out and spoke rapidly in k'iché, waving her arms and looking back at us in the van. One guard came over to Rodolfo, spoke in Spanish, saying we would be allowed 30 minutes, María would get her weavings, we were to park and stay put. No arguments.

After what seemed forever, she returned, aided by her two daughters with an armload of "huipiles." They were beautiful (both Amy and I had seen many, the best at that Weaving Cooperative in San Cristóbal de las Casas in Chiapas, Mexico in 1973 and 1974). Amy explained that we could not buy many for it was the beginning of the trip but would choose two favorites and pay her whatever she asked, no bargaining. María seemed to do some "ciphering" in her head and said 50 quetzales. We gave her 100. She said, "No, that is not fair. We are all honest in our dealings and 50 is more than enough." "Está bien, qué tal si los otros 50 se quedan como 'depósito' por otros dos dentro de unos dias?" ["Fine. What if the other 50 remain as a 'deposit' for two more 'huipiles' in a few days?] María said she and the girls would be in the plaza outside the Capitanía Building in Antigua in two days, so she could find two more really nice ones for us. We agreed on a meeting at 2 p.m. at the "Fuente" in front of the Colonial Palace. In person contact was the only way to see María; no telephone or even dependable mail existed. I did ask one favor, "María could we have a 'plática' of an hour or so and you could teach us and explain to us a bit more of your life?" She smiled, glanced over at the guards, and whispered, "Sí, pero solo en Antigua en el mercado."

We smiled, nodded goodbye and both of us hoped the guards did not confiscate her 100 quetzales (María had tucked the five 20 - quetzal bills deep into a pocket somewhere in her huipil). Rodolfo got us back on the asphalt and main highway down to Antigua in just another 15 minutes or so. He thought this was a good first encounter and he said there would be many more such chances in coming days. The terrain changed slightly the next two hours, gradually losing altitude from the highland down to a mid – way agricultural zone, incredibly rich in color and variety of plants, trees and we saw our first coffee plantations just outside of Antigua. We stopped for a late lunch at one of the major plantations which had opened for tourist visits and offered Guatemalan "hospitality," I presumed to bring in more $$$.

It was called "Cafetzal Antigueño" [Antigua Coffee Plantation] and Rodrigo knew the family that ran it (we would find he seemed to know everyone, "all the right people," ha ha). One of the foremen took us for a short walk and my head was spinning with all the information. I thought coffee was coffee, period. And by the way, I was indoctrinated drinking those wonderful demitasse "cafezinhos" in Brazil for many years.

He first showed us the small trees that looked like bushes to me and then the surprise: "The best coffee in the world comes from right here, and there is a good reason. For our high-quality beans, the coffee bushes must have a mixture of the right soil, moisture, sun, and shade. That is why before an owner even begins to think about coffee trees, he has to plant the shade trees, in this case jacaranda. After about eight years he has the shade canopy and then plants the coffee trees. If all goes well in three or four years, they are producing and will continue to produce for many years."

"Come on inside the café – bar and we'll show you." Then came the second surprise, totally different from Brazil: on each table was a small porcelain pitcher of what they called "esencia de café." Our cups were filled with steaming water and then the "mesero" poured "just the right amount" of the coffee essence in the cups. He spooned in about three spoonsful of the local, brown, organic sugar, also a product of Guatemala, cautioned us to not sip too soon so as to not burn ourselves, and then taste. He did not move but just stood by the table.

"Díos mío, that is good! Wow!" And I discovered soon enough that if you drank too much too late in the day, no sleep that night! We indeed got a 5 p.m. "pick me up." They gifted us with small packages of the beans, still unground, but saying to be sure and bring our Adventurers should the trip take place. This was just one of many kinds of offers by entrepreneurs who were aware of the purpose of our visit. We thanked them profusely and were on our way, Rodrigo thinking hotel check in and dinner would be soon enough. It was kind of a rush into town, down the cobblestone streets and to the hotel. "No se preocupen, mañana habrá tiempo para todo" ["Don' worry, there will be time for everything tomorrow"]. I do want to say that probably no less than six other coffees were introduced to us in just the few weeks of the trip, and I can't pick the best.

Due to the hour Rodolfo drove us down that main street, still cobblestoned with the arch overhead (rumor has it that it provided a means of, heh heh, a "rendezvous" between nuns and priests who happened to live across the street from each other in respective convents and monasteries, circa 1570). He pulled into the broad cobblestoned courtyard of the "Posada de Don Rodrigo," which turned out to be a great choice for our time in Antigua, all harking back to the glory days of the colony in 16th to 18th centuries. The sculpted stone guest entrance with the lions on each side could only remind of old Castille.

We were not that tired but decided that some careful planning for the next day or two would be wise, and it was getting close to dusk, so we stayed in the Posada. There were drinks on the patio, and dare I say, more marimba. I loved it and it made me want to dance, but Amy said to cool it for now. Business to attend to. We did have drinks and listened to many now familiar tunes.

Good ole' Gaherty. I got a pretty good peck on the hand by getting too close to the brilliantly colored red and blue macaws to the right of the band. And to make matters worse, the picture of the birds turned out blurry. There was time however to make notes of our first days in Guatemala and plan for this jewel of the days of conquest and early colony, days by the way not all rosy. We pretty much agreed on our respective "takes" so far. National Palace - Check. 3D Relief Map – might as well; it's on the way. Jean Francoise's - Double Check. National Cathedral – probably not. Kaminaljuyu and Archeological Musium – option for Maya archeology lovers. Maya Clothes washing "Pila" in the country – definitely. Posada de Don Rodrigo – so far, so good.

I might add that the "so far, so good" has a small footnote to it. At the Posada's delightful Yum Kax restaurant while enjoying something terrific and chocolaty for dessert a rather handsome young gentleman in coat and tie came up to our table, apologized profusely for the introduction, but said he had no choice but to introduce himself. It turned out to be Estéban Weissmann from Buenos Aires. He was a regular client at the Marriott years ago when Amy worked at the hotel for a two year sojourn in the days before AT. She seemed a bit flustered at first, but quickly recovered, and asked me if it would be all right if Estéban joined us for an after dinner drink. Okay.

It turned out he was on a "trade mission" from Argentina to Guatemala (and then Mexico) purportedly in Guatemala to deal with the exchange of Guatemalan coffee for Argentinian beef, he heading the first negotiations through the respective Departments of Agriculture. Amy would tell me later his family goes way way back among the "hacendados" of the huge beef "estancias" in the famous Pampa region of Argentina. I guess what's good for Argentina is good fo the Weissman ranches! There was small talk about respective lives after Buenos Aires, Amy first in Rio and now a veteran at AT, he a businessman and export – import specialist. Amy did introduce me, a Professor at the University of Nebraska and cultural lecturer now for AT, and our current project scoping out Guatemala for a new trip. It was all very courteous, lots of laughter of the "good ole days" and he begged pardon for moving on but did leave his business card (ha!) for both of us.

Later in the room I dared to ask Amy if I got the complete story. She smiled, hesitated, and said, "Well, almost. We dated a bit in Buenos Aires, but nothing came of it, but aren't you the guy with a girl in every port? I'm sure I haven't heard all those stories." Touché! Amy said, "Come over here and let's get to know each other again and forget all those stories from the past." We managed to maneuver a bit on those single beds (standard) in the tourist hotels, and I must say, it indeed was like old times. After we were rested, leaning on our pillows and each having a glass of wine I asked, "Amy, why did you call it off?" She said, "Because this is much better, no strings, no obligations, but great friends and co – workers and travelers, what do you think?" How could I argue?

# 3

---

# A LITTLE BIT OF HISTORY
# BUT NOT TOO MUCH

The next a.m. after what would soon be the standard Guatemalteco breakfast – tortillas, fried eggs and black beans, fried plantain (ugh), tasty cheese, and wonderful "café con leite" – we were dressed and with notebooks, pens and cameras in tow met Rodolfo in the tiny park in front of the entrance to the Posada. He said, "We need to go where it all started, so let's make the short drive to Almolongo." Okay. Simple. No, not so simple. Rodolfo says Almolongo in what they call "Ciudad Vieja," today a district of Antigua, was actually the second capital of Guatemala. The first was Santiago de los Caballeros (today's Tecpán) near the old Kakchiquel Maya capital of Iximché, all in the beautiful western highlands near the provinces of Chimaltenango and Sacatepéquez. Here's the thumbnail sketch.

## IXIMCHÉ ARCHEOLOGICAL SITE

The Villa de Santiago de los Caballeros, the town known as Tecpán today, is near the post – classic Maya town of Iximché which is a small archeological site today but was the capital of the post - classic Kaqchiquel Mayas from 1470 to 1524. The Kaqchiqueles were of the K'iché Maya language group. The inhabitants actually offered to ally themselves with the Spanish "conquistadores" who arrived in 1524 in the person of Pedro de Alvarado – the reason was so the Iximché people could help the Spaniards to pacify the Kaqchiqueles' rivals the Quiché in the highlands. There later was a falling out and a Maya attack on the new Spanish capital nearby, Santiago de los Caballeros. The Mayas were defeated and abandoned Iximché; the Spanish burned it two years later and moved the capital to Ciudad Vieja in November of 1527. The eventual Capitanía de Guatemala was important on the route for the Manilla Galleons bringing goods and riches from the Philippines to Acapulco across Mexico to Vera Cruz and on to Spain.

Whew. I told Amy that I, the son of a Nebraska farm boy growing up riding on tractors, did ride horseback with friend Val back in 1962 to the Iximché ruins, not even beginning to realize then their historic importance. I did remember the saddle sores. And the green beauty of the place. The "pyramids" seemed small, not much after seeing Teotihuacán in Mexico weeks earlier.

Anyway, Almolonga (Ciudad Vieja) didn't last long, just 14 years. There was good news and bad news: first the good, the new capital was located in an incredibly beautiful valley on the southwest slope of nearby Volcán del Água. The bad news: the volcano erupted in 1541 and literally emptied its insides, full of water and mud, flooding and destroying the old town. The governor, Beatriz de la Cueva, surviving wife of Conquistador Pedro de Alvarado, had ruled for a time before the flood, but was killed as a result of it. Her brother Francisco da la Cueva and the leading churchman in the area Bishop Francisco de Marroquín ruled in the interim and decided after the devastation to move the capital to the more hospitable spot, today's Antigua. But before the devastation they built a church.

La Iglesia de la Concepción is believed to be in the original "barrio" of Ciudad Vieja, the living area of the Mexican indigenous "allies" Pedro de Alvarado brought with him from Tenochtitlán and were part of the fighting force to overcome the Mayas in Guatemala. The huge edifice was modeled on the church of the "Virgen de la Soledad" in Oaxaca and has some similarities; it is called "Guatemalan Baroque" by the guides. Amy and I couldn't see any of that because when we were there the interior was still closed from the earthquake of 1976, but the exterior, cracked and all, was still impressive. We kept hearing the mantra, "We will fix everything from the earthquake. After all, it's not the first time." The two huge bell towers make an impression.

We would discover that most of central and western Guatemala was damaged if not destroyed completely in 1976, but with some miraculous exceptions. We would have to evaluate all this for the possible AT upcoming trip, but our first impressions were to stay in the countryside, more soon on this. In the Antigua countryside was San Antonio Águas Calientes and Rodolfo said it was so close, best to see it now; he said the weaving was spectacular. So we went.

Like everywhere, it seemed the town of about 5000 people had been devastated by the quake and they were still rebuilding. The textile market was temporarily housed in a wood fenced thatched area, but the weavings were magnificent as Rodolfo promised. After bargaining and always giving a generous fair price, Amy brought two to the van.

Another story was the main church, absolutely devastated; the picture is my file picture from 1976 and restoration was well under way, now three years later.

We did see when rain came later that soggy afternoon that community spirit had not died, the parade of the "gente alta" or "los gigantes" the locals termed it. I'm sorry I don't know more, but it was accompanied by marimba music, drums, and yes saxophones! And we would learn later it was celebrated in almost all the Indian villages of Guatemala at differing times of the year. Another even stranger bit of worship was all the home-made shrines to MAXIMON. More later.

Best of all was the chance encounter with some Guatemalan Maya Indian ladies and their children on the way to the town square to sell textiles. We bought one or two wall hangings, woven in the local style, Amy commenting this purchasing would have to stop for a lack of room in luggage. Yet we were just getting started. We both agreed that the beauty of the countryside and of the people were casting their spell on us. So far, much less, the so-called "monuments." That may change according to Rodolfo, tomorrow in Antigua. I daresay we both, Amy and I, had delightful exchanges in Spanish with every weaver we met.

I'm trying to not be maudlin, but this and many scenes like it were what moved us emotionally and once or twice brought tears to our eyes in these days. We both recalled the promise to María from the Pila on the way to Antigua, and that was scheduled for the next day, our main foray into the town of Antigua itself.

It had been a big day, so we were happy to return to the Posada, sit in the patio bar with drinks and hearing their marimba band once again, and pondering what we had seen. In sum, neither of us was prepared for the devastation we saw today at Almolonga and San Antonio Águas Calientes; the Cathedral in Guatemala City had been severely damaged, but nothing compared to today. Amy wondered if all was going to be like this? If so, for sure AT would not want to do the trip. The concierge at the Posada assured us that Antigua fared much better, this due to the construction techniques learned from the 16th and 17th centuries experience, in short, huge meters - wide walls on many of the main buildings. We would see tomorrow.

I could not begin to keep the Maya weavings straight, both of us having been told there is a specific pattern for each ethnic group, and even each town within a group. There is a famous textile museum in Guatemala City that we were told *must* be on our priority list for Adventurers, but perhaps at the end of their trip to "put things in perspective." We planned to see it before leaving. Amy recalled the Weavers Cooperative in San Cristóbal de las Casas in Chiapas, hoping it would be like that. We would discover, how can I say this, that there exists a certain snobbishness to put it bluntly among weaving aficionados – older "huipiles" with old patterns being highly prized, but an entire pecking order on any of them. We bought a brightly illustrated book which helped a bit, but I never did get a clear view of the matter. The truth? I liked them all.

So with the "history" of Guatemala's second capital of Almolonga tucked in our pocket and noted in the diaries, we would sink our teeth into the "jewel" of it all in Antigua the third capital, beginning tomorrow. I must say, Amy and I as well were feeling more comfortable with each other vis a vis that long hiatus since 1977 in Portugal and Spain, I think in part because there was no pressure. We knew where we stood and stand. On the other hand, I admitted privately to Amy that we should keep an open mind to the future. Once again, "Okay."

That night we finally got into something I salivated over – Guatemala's version of "churrasco" meat cooked over a spit, almost Brazilian style. And luscious lettuce, tomato and avocado salad in this the land of truck farms. I neglected to mention the agriculture on the countryside on the way to San

Antonio, every square inch of land planted. The soil is volcanic, rich and "grows anything."

We were told that the smaller plots generically called "milpas" were owned and farmed by indigenous cooperatives, but I would discover that that was just part of the story. "Milpa" means corn field, and there is a Guatemala "ladino" or white man's joke about them: "Did you hear the story of the Indian who got drunk on 'huaro' and fell out of his cornfield?" Deciphering the text: "huaro" is strong sugar cane liquor -aguardiente - and the milpas are often on the side of steep hills. I think the reader gets the picture. I had only sampled the stuff once, this with friend Val on the beach at Puerto San José on the Pacific. It was clear, looked like water, but one sip burning all the way down was enough.

# 4

## NEXT DAY ANTIGUA

So, now for our big day in Antigua. The reader already knows it was the third, no less, capital of the Capitanía de Guatemala, after Santiago de los Caballeros (Iximché) and Almolonga. The capital was moved from Almolonga to the present site of Antigua in the Panchoy Valley in 1541 after the devastation of the flood of Volcán del Água. Originally all the area was called the Kingdom of Guatemala for 200 years until independence from Spain. Antigua was five miles from old Almolonga, founded by the conquistadores with the same name of Santiago de los Caballeros the first capital at Iximché (the name came from the original date of the battle when the Spaniards defeated the Mayas in Iximché, the day of St. James, Santiago Mata Moros). The Kingdom then constituted most of Central America plus Chiapas. Guatemala had become the head of the "Real Audiencia de Guatemala" in 1549. There were political problems, but in 1570 the Kingdom was established independent of Mexico and now simply was known as the "Audiencia de Guatemala."

The town or city was built over decades, largely due to religious orders. The Franciscans came first. Their cathedral was started with stones from Almolonga, but it suffered continuous earthquakes until 1574. Soldier Bernal Díaz de Castillo of the battle of Tenochtitlán fame in Mexico was buried there. The earthquakes continued in all the 1600s.

The Jesuits came in 1608 and soon established their first school, San Lucas of the Society of Jesus. It was famous in its day for literature and grammar. And later they purchased the site of what would become the San Carlos Borromeo University, a magnificent place now an art museum.

Another major order, the Friars of San Juan de Dios, came in 1636 and were in charge of all hospitals.

So, enough of history for the moment and I think I had it all confused in spite of Rodolfo's tutelage. He said we had to start in the central plaza with the "Palacio de los Capitanes Generales de Guatemala." So we did.

It was the headquarters of the "Real Audiencia de Guatemala" until the 18th century when the capital was moved once again, and the same causes: no end of earthquakes. This place had been rebuilt more than once, most recently in 1764 nine years before the massive earthquake. It was the site of the "Real Audiencia de Guatemala" also called the "Capitanía General del Reino de Guatemala." The leader's title is a mouthful: "Gobernador, Capitán General y Presidente de la Real Audiencia." We would tell any Adventurers of Spain's Viceroyalties, 4 of them, in Nueva España (Mexico),

Peru, Nueva Granada (Venezuela, Colombia and Ecuador) and Río de la Plata (Argentina and the Southern Cone). The Captaincies were smaller, on their borders, but with equal ruling powers within their own region: Cuba, Guatemala, and Chile.

It was easy to see the Spanish had followed their colonial model for such places; we had seen similar sites in Colombia, Mexico and Lima, Peru.

I'm not showing the cathedral of Antigua mainly because after the most recent quake it was not a pretty sight, but it had once been considered the most beautiful building of the capital. It was begun by ole' Bishop Marroquín in 1543 and not finished until 1680. Conquistador Pedro de Alvarado and his wife Beatriz de la Cueva were buried there, but the tombs not yet available to see.

For me the most impressive place that first day was the old University of San Carlos Borromeo, now an art museum. Its history is colorful. Bishop Francisco Marroquín wanted a university for "educación superior" [university level] and got approval of the Pope for the "Santo Tomás de Aquino School" way back in 1543. In 1676 the king of Spain granted rights to the school but now with the name "La Universidad Real de San Carlos Borromeo." It became the best in Guatemala, modeled on the University of Mexico and the renowned University of Salamanca in Spain. In 1773 after one earthquake and another, the capital of Guatemala was moved to today's Guatemala City and the university as well. It was later secularized and became simply "La Universidad de San Carlos.' The building in Antigua remained, at museum since the Jesuit order was thrown out of Spanish possessions in 1767.

It was time to go back to the central plaza in front of the Capitanía Palace where there is a beautiful park and central fountain. Sure enough our new friend Maria and one of her daughters were there as promised.

We bought lunch from vendors in the plaza, and ice cream for her daughter and young friends.

María expressed thanks once again for our help earlier in her village, and we had some time to talk. She seemed reticent at first, saying she could not really say all she wanted with the children present, but did tell us how bad the violence had been the past few years with many men just disappearing from her village, most traveling to "El Norte." She and her husband were surviving, even after the huge quake of 1976, he doing the farm labor on the haciendas down on the Pacific coast, she doing weaving each day. She was convinced to tell us more about her house, realizing the men of the village would not allow us to visit (if it were known we were friends, there could be consequences). She said it was of mud wattle, sticks making up the walls, a tin roof since the quake, earthen floor, and no heat except a small propane camp stove they also cooked on. And of course, no water; that had to be brought in jars from the central "pila." She did say the country was gradually being reconstructed, and some tourists were returning. She said she could not say more nor give us details to reach her, only that she would always be in that plaza on Sundays for the market.

María then unwrapped what turned out to be two dazzling "huipiles" - "The best we have to offer" – all with a big smile, and handed them to us. I don't have the details on the weaving or the patterns other than that María said each took about one full month of weaving to complete. Amy gave María a big hug and said, "Senhora, these are priceless; we will always treasure them." Amy and I agreed to once again leave several large "quetzales" notes with María who at first tried to refuse them, but after we expresed our sincere hopes for her and her family, put them in a woven handbag. We agreed that we would one day meet again in that very plaza.

Rodrigo told us later that her story is common; we would see more examples of the same in the highlands at El Lago de Atitlán and its surrounding towns and in Chichicastenango the major highland market town. For now he wanted to show us just two or three more places in Antigua before we moved on, the old "Recolección" area with ruins of the 18th century quakes, two 16th century convents and two churches which had survived the quakes, La Merced and San Francisco. He thought we could do all that the next morning. So we were left once again at the Posada Don Rodrigo our hotel.

Over drinks with Rodolfo, our guest and "mentor" and gradually becoming a good friend, we digested all we had seen today and tried to assimilate all the dates and facts to make sense of this the best example extant of colonial Guatemala. Frankly I welcomed a change of subject, so we discussed what he promised would be a very different Guatemala in a day or two, the low, wet, tropical lowlands and massive sugar cane plantations and citrus groves' region of the country as well as its "land locked port" of San José on the Pacific. I mentioned nature for the first time, a desire to see a real Quetzal bird and other birds and animals. Rodolfo smiled and said, "Paciencia, veremos todos dentro de unos dias."

It was gradually becoming clearer what AT agent Nataniel Schmidt in Guatemala City had said – that Guatemala in many ways is just a much smaller version of Mexico, albeit with all the differences. We talked of some of this. The terrain, the land and subsequent fertility of the volcanic soil in Guatemala, was just partially visible in Mexico, perhaps from Oaxaca south, southwest and east into Chiapas. The latter of course was once part of the "Capitanía de Guatemala" and its mountainous terrain, volcanic subsoil and Maya peoples were closely related to the same in Guatemala. But central Mexico and on north were much more of a parched land or a mix of wet and dry seasons. One huge difference was gold and silver. And with huge circumstances or at least variants: the indigenous population of Mexico was in effect enslaved to work on the mines of Zacatecas and the Sierra Nevada, but no less a fate faced the Maya in Guatemala on the haciendas of the descendants of the "conquistadores" and favorites of the Crown of Castille.

What was the same was that the indigenous peoples were gradually stripped of most of their lands, first through conquest, then through skullduggery, a very thorny subject. Whatever one thinks of the "cross" of the conquest ["la espada y la cruz" - the conquistadores and the church], the forced conversion of the Indian masses to Catholicism, and the protected role of the Catholic Church for almost 400 years (until the liberalism and anti – church sentiments of the 19th and 20th centuries in most countries) it was the churchmen who protected the Indians from even worse. Padre Bartolomé de las Casas (of fame of the famous debate in Valladolid in Spain defending the basic humanity of the Indians) had served many years before his short stint in San Cristóbal in Mexico in the northeastern province of Cobán in Guatemala. And the Jesuit "Missiones" in Brazil and Paraguay until 1767 are good examples.

Over drinks I explained to Amy that it had always been the Indigenous countries of the Americas that fascinated me most in the years of graduate study in Spanish and early travel – Mexico, Guatemala, Colombia, and Peru to a limited extent, but also the Catholicism of such places (Gaherty! Irish – Amerian! - Catholic family!) Yet, I was never inclined to become an activist in the causes of missionaries or Cathlolic charities, perhaps because the thrust of the graduate degree was to teach others of the language and cultures of America and to prepare them for the capitalist – communist conflict. I dunno. I had my head in the sand most of those years, either in the effort to get the advanced degree or to keep my job by publishing. Maybe the cliché is applicable, a lover, not a fighter. No excuses. The point is Guatemala was bringing all the above back to me. "And by the way, I would not have met you Amy, other wise."

She said, "What about Brazil?" I took a deep breath and a long sip of scotch and went on a bit. Brazil was a different story, altogether different, and the reader will just have to peruse the book on AT travel there, incidentally, when I met Amy. I can say it was the "cool" sound of Brazilian portuguese language, the music and film "Black Orpheus," and an accident in academia that bought it on - the broadsides of the "literatura de Cordel" in a class on Brazilian literature at Georgetown. All that plus being young, red – blooded and wanting to see the biquinis on Copacabana Beach and experience Carnival. But I digress. I don't know what the intellectuals call it, but there were two realities and interests, Spanish and Portuguese, and we're now in Guatemala.

We both came to the same question: what can we do about it all? And we agreed that in our own small way if we could educate first and then have the prosperous Adventurers of AT see first hand this reality and also contribute monetarily to the people they would meet (we were thinking primarily of the Maya women and their weavings), that was not nothing. The reader may recall the plan negotiated for AT travel in Mexico as a result of our preliminary wonderful but harrowing trip before the 1974 AT trip – a plan to actually get $$ into the hands of the maids, the cooks, the guides, all the natives AT travelers would come into contact with. And that might just be the beginning with some of them, future philanthropists back home.

We wondered how anyone, Spaniards included, could come, conquer, but remain in a land where at any given moment all they had done and built could be smashed in hours by an earthquake, and in effect was and still is, 500 years later. And their lives snuffed out in an instant. Amy wondered if it was any different from forest fires, tornadoes, and devastating floods creating victims in the U.S. but we both agreed that was just a similarity, a trifle as it were, to the land of the smoking volcanoes. Her experience in Guatemala was far more limited than mine, but we both marveled, oohed and aahed at the beauty we had seen so far, and even this quake plagued paradise of nature around Antigua.

# 5

## ANTIGUA – THE CHURCHES

That next morning Rodolfo was at our breakfast table and with a big itinerary – the religious side of Antigua. We drove first to the "Recolección," the monastery of the "Recolets" a french branch of the Franciscans started in the 1600s and abruptly destroyed in the immense final earthquake of 1773 that drove the Real Audiencia to finally move to the present day site of Guatemala City. I'm not a fan of ruins per se, but there was a tranquility about the place and one could imagine its original grandeur. You walk through the huge archway of the former entrance and then just see chunks of stones that formed its walls. As difficult it it is to imagine, the last earthquake of 1976 did even more damage.

La Merced was started in 1749 and finished in 1767 and profited from the experience of yet another earthquake in 1751. The architect figured low height, wider arches and columns would save the day, and they did. I had never heard of the Mercedarians, but this edifice is due to the Friars of La Merced Order and was the first monastery for males erected in Antigua. Their origin is the Order of the Blessed Virgin Mary of Mercy, dating from the 13th century! Despite the opposition of the friars, the Real Audiencia required them to move the monastery to Guatemala City after the 1773 quake, along with the famous images, but the entire narthex of the church today is famous for the beginning of the Holy Week Processions in Antigua. The latter are a whole other story and Antigua is famous for them, a Guatemalan "ladino" and "indigenous" version of Holy Week in Sevilla, España. The exterior was incredible, the best we had seen in Guatemala; the interior was rather plain, as mentioned, its famous images moved to Guatemala City. This would not be the case at the Iglesia de San Francisco to come.

For whatever reason San Francisco weathered the recent 1976 quake. It goes back to the mid - 1500s, was destroyed at least twice in the following two centuries and rebuilt once again in the 20th, what you see in the photo.

There was a famous school connected with it and it played an important part during the colony. The Franciscans, by the way, were the first religious order named and allowed to work in the Kingdom of Guatemala and the first in Antigua, basically from the beginning to now. The church houses the shrine in honor of Pedro de San José Betancur, missionary and saint, the main reason for religious pilgrimage and ex-votos for his miracles. And San Francisco is also known for its special attention to the Virgin Mary and the Immaculate Conception.

During our visit we saw some truly memorable images etc. in the church, so I have several photos. The "Virgen Pastora" and "Jesus carrying the cross" indeed are worthy of future Adventurers' attention. Amy and I both marveled at the robes adorning these Catholic effigies, and we wondered where the gold came from for that cross. Amy said, "Jesus has certainly come a long way from the wood of the true cross!" (And I added, "All the relics, in handy sliver size."). I felt a need to respond that María la Virgen must have been moved by the shepherds at Bethlehem, but I think maybe someone got a bit carried away; Jesus after all was the "Buen Pastor." The Franciscans were keeping it in the family, I guess. But both images are incredibly beautiful and deserve the prayers.

The chapel dedicated to the missionary – Saint Pedro Betancur, for us immediately recalling the "Igreja do Bonfim" in Salvador da Bahia, Brazil, and its miracle room with all the "ex -votos" - plastic heads, arms, hands, and such as proof of cures and the answering of the petitions of the faithful. Bahia had its photos as well. I am proud of the accidental nature of the photo showing obvious well – to – do tourists, local or otherwise, but mainly the Maya ladies behind them. I hope prayers were answered.

And finally, the local children were there with their wares trying to earn a quetzal or two. We gave them both generous donations, asking for just a smile in return. In retrospect, the girl on the left with no shoes says more than many words.

I thought we were done, but Rodrigo said, "Just one more stop. We can't forget the "monjas" [nuns]. It was back near the town center where we saw the ruins of two major nunneries, the Santa Clara and more important for us, the Las Capuchinas Convent.

The locals call it "El Convento de las Capuchinas." Rodolfo says more accurately it is the convent of the Clarissa Nuns dating from 1522 in Naples, Italy. Things went well for them, Claire their founder related to St. Francis, and sometime later they were in Spain. Later, in 1538, a religious order called "Orden de las Hermanas Clarisas Capuchinas" arrived in Antigua (an offshoot of the Franciscans). Surviving those years of volcano and earthquake disaster they started this convent in 1726 and finished it in 1736. The official name is a mouthful: "Convento e Iglesia Nuestra Señora del Pilar de Zaragoza." They call the architectural style "earthquake baroque" because of the lower ceilings and thick walls. So, all were learning from Antigua's past. Just 25 nuns were living there at our time, cloistered, known for their singing at mass which they did from a curtained "celosia" up in the back of the church.

So, it's memories for Amy and me. And, ahem, maybe for a reader or two: when AT did the trip to Portugal and Spain back in 1977 aboard the "International Adventurer," we of course visited Zaragoza and saw that incredible Basilica dedicated to the Virgen and to St. James "Santiago Mata Moros." I don't know the nuns' connection to Zaragoza, but expect they had a convent there as well.

Okay. Here we go again. "Voy a Zaragoza a comer cigalas en la plaza de Zaragoza." Pronounce like a Castilian please. Someone once said and I quote, "Spanish is like Portuguese but with a speech impediment." I highly suspect it was a Portuguese. I didn't think I could write that in this book. I had a Spanish professor at Georgetown who hated Portuguese but admitted after an evening with quite a few glasses of "clarete" that he really could just not get the hang of it. Amy was with me on all these jokes, knowing a lot of both languages.

Don't get me started. Okay, get me started. Teaching both Spanish and Portuguese, and, ahem, being pretty good at it, I have strong opinions on this subject. Suffice to say: in many years of personal contact with educated native Spanish speakers, they say it is quite easy to learn Portuguese (I never found one motivated to do so) and educated Portuguese speakers in

Brazil say the Spanish of the Americas is very much like their language and also easy to learn (I found few motivated to do so, and with only a few exceptions, disproving the theory). All right, here it is: my best students of Portuguese were Anglos, but only those very highly motivated and with a gift ("don") for language. The others could not keep the two languages straight. (I await the onslaught of rotten cabbages and tomatoes.) Another topic is which country in the Americas has the "best" Spanish.

Rodolfo said the final moments in town had to be up on the hill with the huge statue of founder "Conquistador Pedro de Alvarado" (the statue looked like one we saw of "El Cid" in old Castille in Burgos, perhaps just a coincidence) but with the still ominous Volcán del Água in the background high above that apparently placid, gorgeous valley.

So we bade goodbye to Antigua for the present, both excited for its prospects for the upcoming trip, but also with reservations. People were still "jumpy" and there were tremors, slight to be sure. The first time we felt our beds move in "La Posada" was downright scary. We were told to not worry about it.

# 6

## ON THE ROAD TO THE PACIFIC AND "PUERTO SAN JOSÉ"

I have never yet seen a place in Guatemala that looks like it could not grow something. Nothing barren, nothing too rocky. We were going to be introduced to yet another green place, but very different from the highlands (and midlands) seen so far. That is the road to the Pacific. Rodolfo said this would now be like the Caribbean, Cuba or the Dominican Republic (or, I said, the northeast coast of Brazil) – sugar cane plantations, tobacco plantations, cattle ranches, but all owned by that tiny minority of wealthy upper class "old rich" Guatemaltecos. I asked about the laborers, being quite familiar with the same in Brazil's northeast (descendants of slaves or poor white sharecroppers). There was probably some black slavery here, but Rodolfo says the area depends far more on seasonal migrant labor from the Indians from the highlands (like María's husband).

The area all seemed so wet and soggy, and yes, incredibly humid; we saw a familiar sight, a big lorry with sugar cane stacked to the top, off to the refinery we presumed. I recall seeing a dump truck about that size driven by a friend of my college buddy Val, the former making "cigarette money" with a load of oranges from the coast up to the market in Guatemala City.

Just a small aside, we stopped at a very poor small town alongside the road and saw "the tree." Rodolfo says it is famous, a minor tourist stop on the way to the coast. The largest "tule" tree in Guatemala. It immediately brought back images of a similar sight we had seen near Oaxaca in Mexico, on the way to the ruins of Mitla.

Neither Amy nor I were impressed with our first view of Puerto San José, or put that another way, the village of San José. It seemed mainly to be small huts in palm groves, lots of small fishing boats and "pirogas" [dugout canoes] and nets. There was one nice ocean front resort called Chula Mar, and Rodrigo and AT had us lodged there. Chula Mar had the standard grass or palm roofed bungalows and central restaurant with pool overlooking the black, volcanic sand beaches and the Pacific, the latter a first for me. The place was not crowded, perhaps that should have been a sign. Still off season, I guess. We were tired from the a.m. sightseeing and the drive but checked in, had a delightful late lunch of broiled garlic shrimp, rice and beans and a margarita, then a nap, and then time for the beach. We would leave for Guatemala City mid - morning tomorrow.

The port of San José was undeveloped and had both of us wondering why. The owner at Chula Mar, clued into the reason for our trip and probably hoping for any tourist business he could get, explained: there is no natural harbor or cove to make a harbor on the Pacific coast of Guatemala, just the long straight beach and open sea. When we later went for a walk and a careful dip in the ocean, we discovered a pier with a long, straight, two – lane causeway built on pilings that led to a small, shed like structure on the end. And we noticed freight trucks carefully making their way to the end of the pier. There were small boats with diesel engines that were used to transport anything and everything from the "port" to large ships anchored out from shore perhaps a mile distant. Not a great scene for export – import! Señor Widemann, the owner of Chula Mar, said there were plans for major dredging and construction for what would be a decent port, but millions of dollars in investment money and probably up to five years in construction were factors in the future. His eyes grew large talking of the possibilities. Amy and I would discuss this later at dinner, offered at no charge by our ambitious host.

So after that lunch we donned swim suits and headed to the beach, but with warnings from Sr. Widemann: "The beach at San José is unique in Central America, beautiful but with black sand, a result of this country seemingly surrounded by volcanoes. However, when that beach is baked by the sun throughout the year but especially in the dry warm season, the sand becomes hot enough to burn the bottoms of your feet. So good sandals are a must. Secondly, there is a fierce undertow all along the beach for miles. One can swim but only taking precautions to not enter the surf more than about twenty meters." He then waxed "Rotarian" in praise of his country: "Volcanoes have made our country unique, and they are beautiful to behold. Our scientists are tops in the world with investigation of them, tours are always available, including to 'live' volcanoes. And in fact, there is a national hobby, we like to call it 'Guatemalan Olympics,' to climb all of them; accounts appear in all the newspapers of a new climb."

Perhaps a bit out of line, I asked Sr. Widemann about his name, surely not Spanish and how did he, obviously of Germanic ethnicity, got to Puerto San José. He laughed and said, "Professor Miguel, the longer you are here the more you will encounter real Guatemalans with German names. You have the same in your country. And I daresay, your own favorite of Brazil and then Argentina. It is not a recent phenomenon, but at least four generations of my people have come here, first of all because of the incredibly rich volcanic soil it offers, with resulting opportunities in the "viña" or grape vineyards, the brewing of stout German beer as a result of the fine harvests of hops and barley, and also because of our own Catholic heritage. From the Holy Roman Empire on, through the Hapsburgs and Austria, there has been a natural link to the Americas. My grandfather came in 1880 and then no less than six of his brothers. Somehow, we all found beautiful, enchanting young ladies to marry, and the Widemanns are famous in all the country. You will encounter our inns and lodges farther on in your travels."

"Sir, indeed, I am somewhat familiar with that Germanic past, especially the Hapsburgs of the 16th century, and once read that Carlos I (Carlos V of Spain) when he was young, had to learn Castilian when he was crowned King of Spain, speaking only German. Is that right?"

"Miguel, I'm happy to say you have done your homework. Well, the afternoon is short, and I understand you are headed back to the city tomorrow, so I hope we can speak to you again at dinner, verdad?"

That p.m. under a partly cloudy sky but with very warm temperatures we did head for the beach, taking all those precautions. It was glorious weather, and the water was refreshing, Amy after these past years was still regaling onlookers with a wonderful, trim, and, okay, sexy body in a bikini. If you have read my past three travel accounts of AT this should be no surprise.

One striking scene (for me anyway) was a huge ocean freighter beached, perhaps permanently, along the shore. We were told there was a horrific storm one year ago, the ship has lost power to its engines and was washed all the way ashore and as of yet, no one could or would come up with the salvage fee or to somehow tow it back to sea. I thought to myself: if these seas and winds can do that, how about unwary tourists? Amy and I would try to assess all this at dinner.

We probably were out only an hour and a half, but that was enough to start a sunburn for me, so we called it an afternoon, walked back up the beach to Chula Mar, had cool showers and some private time, and then prepared for a nice dinner and talk on the veranda of the Chula Mar Inn of the wonderful day. Or at least it started that way.

First came the talk with Sr. Widemann; he knows the Meier family (my host family in Guatemala City and Válter or "Val" for short, my buddy at Creighton in Omaha) I repeated all that story of 1962 to him. He said the Meier family was instrumental in building the pier at San José, that one of the Meier brothers owned fishing boats, and said if you do not know all the German families in Guatemala, you at least are familiar with their names; the Meiers stay at Chula Mar when in the town for business or pleasure at San Jose.

Wolf (his first name) also talked of his sister's lodge at Lake Atitlán and said he would set up a special stay and rates with her if so desired. Amy nodded, why not? He added it is the choice accommodation other than "La Casa Contenta," but then Wolf has an interest in that as well. It's a small world, I guess.

Señor Widemann talked of the contrast between Puerto San José and Puerto Barrios on the Atlantic, the latter, a major, profitable, "going concern." Amy mentioned she knew of it because AT would dock there and run short trips up to Tikal and then Belize for the Adventurers on Atlantic expeditions.

Now to the dinner. First there was an appetizer of huge grilled prawns, and then we were urged to try oysters with a shot of "good" huaro ("Las ostras son las mejores de todo Guatemala y el huaro una especialidad de nuestra propia bodega"). I hesitated at first, but the recommendation was coming after all from the owner. The oysters, just four of them, went sliding down, and the "huaro" was actually tasty and without that sharp burning of the "common" stuff (I think ours was not the usual vintage imbibed by the Maya). We had a wonderful dinner of baked sea bass, garlic rice and vegetables, accompanied by wines and beer from the Widemann wineries and distilleries. And a chocolate – cocoanut pastry to kill for, and of course wonderful coffee.

So what was it that brought in the middle of the night the worst abdominal pain and cramps and subsequent "turista" I had ever experienced in my life? Whoa. Moctezuma was 1000 miles north in Mexico and I did not know the local name in Guatemala, but I'm thinking the local "venganza" [revenge] was making up for Pedro de Alvarado's misdoings during the conquest. I was up the rest of the night back and forth from the "baño" to the bed, fortunate that we had comfortable facilities. Woozy the next morning and barely glued together with the last of my Pepto tablets, Rodolfo drove us at what seemed breakneck speed back to Guatemala City and a specialist recommended by a chagrinned Wolf Widemann. The latter had apologized profusely, visibly distraught over the discomfort of his new friend and possible future clients. (We would talk about that later.) Amy was apparently successful in assuring him that such a thing could not possibly have been his fault. (Whose then, Miss Amy?)

We were rushed into Dr. Müller' office (where in the hell am I, Bavaria?). There was no doubt in his mind after a description of the symptoms of the last twelve hours, a physical examination, and pardon me, a feces test, that I indeed had contracted amoebic dysentery. His explanation was that since the 1976 earthquake the malady had spiked in the country, among all ethnic groups and social classes. "The entire system of water supply, pipes, storage tanks, faucets, etc. was broken by the tremors, and is thus susceptible to the problem. And only part of it has been fixed. Miguel, were you drinking bottled water exclusively the last 24 hours?"

I said, "Not hardly. We had beer, wine, even 'huaro,' and I had a scotch or two at cocktail hour before dinner." "Was it neat or did you have ice?" Gulp. "Uh, with ice of course, but it was from the kitchen of Chula Mar." He frowned and said, "That probably was the culprit. But it could have been a glass washed with contaminated water or even from a wine or beer bottle. Everyone does their best, and my friend Wolf Widemann certainly would take no chances. This is definitely one case that slipped between the cracks. Mike, the good news is you do not have hepatitis; it is now rampant in Guatemala for the same reasons."

Amy was looking at me with that dagger look. "Why in hell were we not informed of all this before we decided to do this trip, Mike?" I was in no shape to debate the matter but just weakly said, "Amy, Mexico is just as bad, or can be. I'm sure they were sugar coating it all to make sure we would travel, and maybe in good faith." She gave me a hug and said, "Possibly, but not likely."

Dr. Müller said he was prescribing something that would definitely take care of the nasty amoebae but urged absolute caution with water and other basics. "You should be better within 48 hours, able to continue your travels. Oh, by the way Mike, have you been drinking any coffee as I suspect?" I said, "Claro que sí. I love the stuff and am addicted to it." He smiled, then said, "For now my friend, no coffee either, you know what it can do. Give it a week. And then I think decaffeinated. Sorry."

You can imagine my state of mind the rest of that day and the next. I was sick but I was also pissed off. Coffee – one of the joys of my life and especially here in Guatemala! We were back at the hotel, me resting, drinking lots of safe bottled water and fruit juice, nothing else. I've written many times of the famous stomach of this gringo, a fact well known to my students who shared my travel adventures in the classrooms at Nebraska and Georgetown. Amy was ready to pack up and leave, but after a visit from Nathaniel Schmidt from AT and Rodolfo at his side, she and I were convinced to give it all a try, … again.

An interesting footnote: When I read the label on the bottle of antibiotics ("etiqueta," the funny word in Spanish) Dr. Muller prescribed, there was another shock, paraphrasing: "Continued use of this product may lead to blindness." Holy shit! I'm not lying. So, take your pick: amoebic dysentery or blindness. I read it again and so did Amy, no mistake. The prescription was for one week, pills twice a day. I also had Rodolfo do an errand: go to the pharmacy and buy a half dozen packages of Pepto Bismol tablets.

We took an extra day at the Hilton, me now on plain cooked white rice and toast. And nothing hot at breakfast. All I can think of are scatological words, but they expressed the emotions, MIERDA!

We had time to talk and plan the next segment of travel, now to the real highlands, past Iximché, a visit to the famous Katok Inn and then to the "Lago de Atitlán," Sololá the town on top, Panajachel at the bottom near the lake and a full three days to really investigate the place. From everything we had read, this should be wonderful!

We did have a bit of a debate over the time in Puerto San José. We both remembered the hot volcanic sand, the rough sea with the warnings of undertow, the primitiveness of much of the area, but maybe that very primitiveness would be a welcome change for Adventurers used to

Acapulco or Rio or even the French Riviera. Amy who suffered not a twit from food or drink at Chula Mar, to the contrary, raved about it all, the beautiful blue pool facing that black beach and wonderful ocean view, thinking it should not be crossed off our list of "potentials." I recused myself. Ha! And of course we had to not think of it in isolation, but as just the final segment of the Antigua, Águas Calientes jaunt. No argument there. Antigua is not only a jewel of Guatemala but all Latin America. Too bad AT could not go during Holy Week, but table that notion.

# 7

## BACK TO THE HIGHLANDS – THE MAGIC OF ATITLÁN

Rodolfo was back as driver, sometime translator, and "illuminator" of this "Holy Book of Guatemala" as he so colorfully put it (think of the "Book of Kells," well, sort of). I was feeling much better, eating things I liked but ran into one problem early in the trip at a stop at the famous restaurant (in Guatemala) on the Pan American Highway high road to El Lago, Katok – spicy smoked sausages, a no, no. I had loved the place back in 1962 when I stopped two or three times with Val Meier on the way back and forth to the lake and to his farm near the town of Tecpán, and also near Iximché Ruins. It was all positive: we rode horseback from the farm to the ruins and were the only ones there! It was not on the major tourist map in those days. More on that soon. Back to Katok.

It was a small-time country inn in 1962, a place to get a bite to eat from the Lake to the city, but now it was a full-fledged tourist stop. It was easy to see why: rustic on the outside with huge palm-fronded roof, beautifully hued logs inside, a kitchen smell that titillated the senses the minute you walked in the door, a full bar and menu. They were famous for their own smoked and barbecued meats, but since it was still mid – morning, we had that Guatemalan breakfast I have talked about: fried eggs on their black corn tortillas, mashed black beans, a big slice of watermelon, and delicious cheese. My stomach could handle it. Amy added the usual that I could not handle: guacamole and two kinds of salsa, red and green, (the menu called it: "huevos divorciados." Ha. The waiters were all congenial and the owner, all right, not a German Guatemalan, Felipe Sánchez, sat with us and told some of the history of the place: his family had the inn for 50 years; he now graciously offered us the best. (He was clued in once again by Rodolfo and the promise of many wealthy foreigners to come, that is, if Amy gave her household seal of approval.) We were told to come back sometime for the big lunch featuring all that beef or pork or chicken, and there would be marimba music to accompany it all. It was an incredibly great introduction (pardon me, the Baroque hyperbole of my Spanish literature studies sometimes overcomes me).

Rodolfo wanted us to be at Lake Atitlán well before dark, anticipating its spectacular scenery, so we put off a drive to Iximché, he assuring us we could stop on the way back from the highlands. It was only about an hour from Katok to the view at the top overlooking El Lago de Atitlán and the glorious coming days. We stopped at the overlook on top and it was like seeing paradise on earth. I had told Amy that back in 1962 when I first came to Guatemala, I thought it was the most beautiful place I had ever seen.

Oops. I said that about my first view of the Pacific Ocean at Acapulco perhaps a full month earlier. I've written of the moment before, but it bears repeating. Being from Nebraska I had never seen the ocean, any ocean, until after the summer school at the Universidad Autónoma de México in 1962 and the bus ride to Acapulco. When the 5 Estrellas Autobús de Lujo came over that last hill through the forest and I saw the blue expanse before me through the palm trees, I thought indeed, I was in heaven. This is why I put up with that 50-hour bus ride from Omaha, Nebraska to Mexico City. My God, it was beautiful!

In 1962 my friend Val brought me to Atitlán the first time, we stayed at the "Casa Contenta" and that first night enjoyed a sumptuous steak dinner with all the trimmings, I heard marimba music for the first time, and I danced with some beautiful, young, Guatemalan young ladies, all upper class and all part of that "clique" the Meiers were part of. Later that night I was introduced to scotch whiskey, Johnny Walker Red, by Val's uncles. Okay.

The lake is landlocked with no rivers or other openings to the sea, although scientists have long thought there was an underground flow to the Pacific. The water level did drop a full two meters after the earthquake of 1976. It is a clear, cold-water lake at about 340 meters in depth! It was formed as the caldera of a volcano long ago and today has three major volcanoes surrounding it to the south, Volcán Atitlán, Volcán San Pedro, and Volcán Tolíman. Intensive fishing has lessened over the years, but Black Bass at one time populated the lake and were a source of food for the natives as well as sport fishing for others. I fished there, unsuccessfully while visiting the lake with friend Val and his family; they all caught fish, I had never handled a Garcia-Mitchell spinning rod. But I learned later!

There are twelve indigenous towns surrounding the beautiful lake, or there were, for volcanic activity and a massive flood has taken its toll on them. These and the greatest problem of all – mankind! I can't avoid it: the ongoing right wing military government in Guatemala in a "scorched earth policy" attacked natives by the lake unmercifully in the 1970s, killing hundreds and driving many away forever. It was "war against the Communists and the subversives." As we drove down the paved road from the top to lakeside we first passed through Sololá, and we saw the remains of machine gun bullets on the church and other buildings in the plaza.

In spite of all this, the view from above and Sololá revealed fields and embankments all around the lake containing rich, volcanic soil. We would see later that the remaining natives farm it intensively, mostly a sort of truck farming of vegetables, but corn as well. After Sololá and Rodolfo filling us in a bit on those bad days, we followed the road on down to the lake where we had decided to spend the first two nights at the iconic Casa Contenta Hotel.

It had been almost twenty years, and one tends to forget, but the moment we walked inside, past the registration desk and into the huge open dining room (log beams everywhere and thatched roof on top) with the gigantic stone fireplace and then the plate glass windows viewing the lake, it all came back. A young 20-year-old in love with Guatemala, in no small way due to the terrific food, the warm, hospitable company, the drinks, the beautiful marimba music and the dancing with those upper class beautiful Guatemalan beauties, most friends or acquaintances of the Meiers. It made my decision to do graduate work in Spanish and specialize in Latin America. I did not necessarily talk of all this to Amy.

We were lodged in, as per the hotel name, one of the Casa Contenta's cottages, and indeed we were "contentos" as a result. I think this was when Amy and I really renewed our old love affair. Surrounded by blooming flowers and with that gorgeous view of the lake, we spent that first evening romancing each other. My stomach could well withstand the filet mignon steak dinner, Amy the "plato guatemalteco de especialidades," two bottles of wine, and I swear, could it be, maybe the sons of the musicians of 1962, playing marimba music. No need to repeat, but yes, Rodolfo had clued in the management of the purpose of our trip, and future reservations by rich gringos gave them the impetus to treat us well. We dined, we drank toasts to each other, and we danced, all before retiring to the fireplace in our "casita." I was back in heaven for the umpteenth time, any Amy too.

Tomorrow our first outing will be the "mail boat" to Santiago Atitlán, way across the lake.

## FIRST DAY AT EL LAGO DE ATITLÁN

We were awake early, had breakfast brought to the room that first morning, and later were out on the patio with all the hyacinth flowers and our coffee and looking at the beautiful front view of the lake. The sun was shining, there were Maya ladies doing their wash down by the water's edge and an occasional "piroga" or dugout canoe going by, the man often trailing a single fishing line in the water.

At 9:00 a.m. we were over to the main dock to catch the "mail boat," not exactly a romantic name but suffice to say it traversed the lake each day stopping at almost all the villages that had a wooden dock. Some did not, and natives in canoes would meet the boat and do a quick and I may say skillful "switcheroo" of mail in and out. The lake is huge, and it took almost one hour to get to our destination, the town of Santiago Atitlán, and well worth it. It was market day and very busy, many families in attendance, and of note, a huge truck filled with the healthiest and best-looking avocados I had ever seen. We were told the volcanic soil plus altitude and climate made for the best avocado plants in all Guatemala. Indian gardens all along the lake had them plus the staple of corn, and vegetables, mainly onions. We would see more of that later if all works out.

This little girl in the above photo was evidently familiar with tourists and said to us in a singsong voice "Take a picher, diez centavos." That is, before her mother stopped her. But when Amy spoke in Spanish that we would respect the image, and had a one quetzal note in her hand, it was allowed. I may have said before, perhaps in Antigua, that the indigenous people we met on this trip believed that a photo of a person captured that person's "soul" and were fearful of the photos. Also interesting is that from previous study of major works on the Maya we saw the stone stelae with all the images of Maya deities; these by and large were defaced on the faces sometime after the major sites were abandoned. A coincidence? Santiago weaving is unique as is the use of the long, wrapped band around the head. Beautiful. The striped blouse and woven patterned skirt of the lady in the background was also the common dress in the market that day.

Time was getting on. It would soon be time get back to the mail boat, the only way out of town until the next day. We were surprised when approached on our way back to the boat; we were corralled by a local shaman insistent there was something else for us to see. (For a price.) He said, "It is our religion."

Perhaps in part. It was Maximón! Not exactly well known in the "Lives of the Saints" in the Catholic church, we found out he was alive and well in the Maya villages around Lake Atitlán. I had heard about him in graduate school at Georgetown from a fellow Ph.D. student from Guatemala. Mário, the son of a coffee plantation owner, albeit, a small farm, had studied at the Jesuit prep school in Belize and ended up doing a B.A. and M.A. at Georgetown during my time. He knew I had been to Guatemala in 1962 and had been to Atitlán, and over beers one day in a watering hole in Georgetown, laughed and laughed and wondered if "Maximón" got me! Mario made him out as more of an indigenous "boogeyman" and said most Guatemalans considered him "local color," "But don't tell that to the Indians in Sololá or Quetzaltenango!"

Led by the shaman, we were able to stick our heads in the doorway of one of the main residences in Santiago Atitlán, with permission from the owner (who had a quick confab with the shaman), resulting in a generous "tip." And his repeating the story the "shaman" told us.

According to folk legend (and Maximón's legend goes back to pre – Spanish, Pre – Columbian days), when the Maya men left their villages to do field work, Maximón would show up and sleep with their wives. When the men found out, they caught him and cut off his arms and legs, leaving behind a "womanizing torso." He was also known for chain smoking and drinking huge quantities of "huaro," a real character. But his effigy is kept in many indigenous homes with a shrine, and he is trotted out (like so many of the "official" Catholic saints in the Maya churches in the highlands) for a "paseo" but, ha ha, not to stretch his legs! And his procession is a mainstay during Holy Week. Back "home" in Santiago de Atitlán his altar has "huaro," cigarettes and even coins as an offering. He may have a cowboy hat and a bandana and sometimes sunglasses! They pray to him like a "mischievous" devil – to stay away from their wives and not steal their children! Some try to pour alcohol down his throat during Holy

Week. (He did not give up alcohol for Lent.) Amy and I thought he was a bit like Exú in Candomblé in Brazil, but a lot more colorful!

After this there was a bit of a rush getting to the Mail Boat, but we barely made it; otherwise, there would have been overnight in who knows what conditions in Santiago. Maybe we missed an adventure. On the way back we saw lots of local piroga travel and one of the many villages alongside the lake, more on that soon.

Soon after this last photo the wind started stirring up, the preamble we were told to the "xocomil" - the high winds and storms that customarily come to the lake in the p.m. Thus is explained the tight schedule the Milk Boat took each day. We were rocking and both of us feeling a bit queasy by the time we landed back at the dock at Panajachel. Whew! I have neglected to say that the pilot had trouble getting the engine to turn over back in Santiago. Food for thought.

Exhausted but happy from all we saw, time for drinks at the Casita to discuss ramifications for AT and then once again dinner, drinks, marimba music and dancing at the main lodge.

Amy and I were in total agreement that this special place on the planet is a "must" for the prospective trip – the scenery coming in, Katok for the food and ambiance, the road down to the lake, Sololá, and the amazing scene itself. The "Casa Contenta" was first rate including the lodge. The mail boat to Santiago Atitlán on market day, the weaving and especially Maximón!

We planned the next day, totally different – a walk and or hike to the east side of the lake to Santa Catarina Palopó and San Antonio Palopó, two of the principal indian villages. Let's see, how many days has it been in Guatemala? Eight, not counting my two "sick" days in Guatemala Cty. Day 9 tomorrow will be the hike.

# THE NEXT DAY

After the now standard "desayuno" of fried eggs, black beans, tortillas, fruit and juice (and my limit, one small cup of real café) we set off on what we hoped would be a real adventure – the essence of El Lago de Atitlán. It was not a far walk from our "casita" to a road through the back of Panajachel, and past "El Rancho" Lodge I'll talk about later. The town was still a hippie haven although many had been "invited" to leave during the military "cleansing" campaigns of recent years. If you were "gringo" they expected you to be "dope heads," but we did not exactly look the part – long hair, and unkempt. It was all a mixture of tropical and sub-tropical: banana trees, small fields of coffee bushes, cabanas and summer small vacation homes on the way out of town. There was a constant stream of Maya ladies, their children and even Maya farmers with animals or crops on the way to market. The day was sunny and just a bit cool; it had rained last night. I would say perfect!

Most of the natives were in their village dress, the accustomed weavings, and we were told it was not just "dress up" for the tourists, but that somehow with all the chaos of past years and hardship, the old customs still prevailed. We had a wonderful conversation, see the coming photo with the man and woman with their two pigs. They were taking them all the way through Panajachel and up the long road to Sololá to the market there. Mike, the old Nebraska farm boy, marveled and thought, imagine in Nebraska taking one, ONE pig to market. Humbling and food for thought when thinking of the precarious economic lives these people led.

And there was a another farm first: a chicken napping on one of those heavy duty hoes the Maya use as both shovel and hoe for planting. This was along the road just after seeing the pigs.

Once we were through the village and its outskirts there was one scary moment, at least for me. To continue the hike, we would have to get across a major, rushing stream, walking on a narrow log, and keeping your balance. It was no problem for gazelle – like Amy, but I had to be cajoled in "taking the leap."

But after that it was so – called smooth sailing, at least for a while, and then an unforgettable few hours where I think we both were able to immerse ourselves into life at the Lake, at least to a limited extent. Our destinations were two "sister" villages, Santa Catarina Palopó and a bit further along San Antonio de Palopó. There was yet another, but you had to get a canoe ride to go there – San Pedro de la Laguna.

After traversing that river coming into the lake side, the trail gradually began to climb and soon we had a spectacular view of the lake on a splendid sunny morning, including all three volcanoes that surrounded it. Have I named them? What caught the ole' farm boy's attention was a fellow bent over, a pan full of something by his side and planting something. No mystery there – it was onions, one of the major crops around the lake. I took the initiative and struck up a conversation with the middle-aged fellow, both of us speaking slowly in Spanish. He was Tacho Max Gómez of Santa Catarina Palopó pueblo which we could see down the incline a bit farther down the shore. He wore a brown felt hat, cowboy style, the blue, white striped shirt, the embroidered pants with bird and flower symbols, white with red stripes, and "huaraches" but made of rubber. I did notice a curiosity – under a jacket and bag with more supplies was a rather large transistor radio! Even Maya farmers are like us folks in Nebraska – you get bored out in the fields! The weather report? Or the latest Maya marimba hits?

The small squares of soil in the midst of rocks were ready for planting the onions, one section obviously recently hoed to break up clods and make the soil smooth. I'm sure the next square would be subject to the same procedure. I explained that my friend and I were visiting his beautiful country and seeing the sights, but were very interested in its history, and particularly the indigenous towns and people. He took some time to look us over and must have made his decision. He smiled and said ironically, "So are a lot of others but not for good reasons. If you promise to not quote me personally and not stray one iota from what I tell you, I can explain." Amy and I both shook our heads yes, maybe we had fallen into a great piece of luck to meet him.

He said, "I don't have too much time because I have to finish this patch today and it is the rainy season; we will have a downpour in about two hours. (I noticed he wore no watch and probably did not need one.) Do you mind if I keep planting as I talk?"

"No hay problema."

"My people have lived in Santa Catarina Palopó for as long as I can remember. I think maybe it could be at least five generations. We as individuals do not own this land, but our clan does, the land grant with the legal title of our village. And we constantly have to fight a battle in court. What is your name? ("Miguel y Amy".) Miguel, the twelve villages around the lake are united in one "Frente Indígena de Tierras Hereditarias" [Indigenous Front of Hereditary Lands] and fortunately there are a few decent "ladinos" including lawyers who help us. You wonder why? Because constantly there are entities trying to steal our land. Some come to the village in a friendly sort of way, smile a lot, and make fairly generous offers for our "milpas." But Miguel, our property, that is, what is left, is not for sale and never will be. But others come with a sheaf of papers in their hands with false allegations that we owe taxes to the "Municipio" of Sololá and to the national government. That would be true if our land were public land or in the "ladino" private domain. But it is Maya and has always been. Our peoples were conquered by the Spaniards 500 years ago, but we never legally ceded this land. But nothing was ever written down save for the land grant documents of years ago, barely readable. That is just one problem. Can you stand to hear more ["Aguentas oír más?"] He said this smiling, a rueful smile to be sure, but not in a raised or angry voice.

"In the past few years and yet today (I include a suggestion you keep your eyes open for your own safety) we have suffered tremendous losses to our lives, our community, and our entire existence here in Guatemala and especially around the lake. In short, there is a national 'cleansing' by the military of any opposition, but especially the left and the communists. The problem is they believe, wrongly I might add, that we indigenous peoples are tied into the left. Nothing could be farther from the truth. We just want peace and quiet for us to continue our lives here and to do what we do best – farm. But the rebels have come in the night and demanded food and sometimes a place to sleep. THAT is why the government soldiers come and shoot at us. Many of us have been killed and more have fled, hoping to get to your country and a better life. My own family has chosen to stay, but we have to be constantly vigilant.

"If that was not enough, we were all devastated by the earthquake of four years ago, you can see the evidence everywhere. We are trying to rebuild and return to what used to be 'normal,' but it has not been easy. Mike and Amy, that is our story."

"Tacho, thank you. We are both moved by your story and believe me, we will try to help in any way we can. I do want you to know in a different vein, that I grew up on a farm in Nebraska in the U.S. and each April my family planted garden and rows of onions like you. The produce was for our table and was not a cash crop. We planted wheat, corn, and alfalfa for that. May I take a picture or two of you planting?"

"Seguro que sí hombre. Si quieres mojar las manos, por qué no plantas unas cebollas de la panela?"

["Sure, señor. If you want to get your hands dirty, why do you not plant some of those seedlings from the pan?"]

I did it, getting a bit muddy in the process, but he had a cloth I used to wipe my hands. Tacho laughed a bit, saying "I think you are out of practice. I could plant five for your time of one!"

"Tacho, can you talk of your harvest and what it brings in?"

"We get six or seven quetzales (6 or 7 dollars) for a thousand onions harvested. You can look around at the size of the gardens and do the math; it's not much. Are you going down to the pueblo? There are many gardens along the shore of the lake as well. Up here our big problem is when it rains too much, it washes everything down the hills. We try to build small dikes to prevent that, but it's an ongoing battle."

Amy had been quiet but spoke up in Spanish telling Tacho how much she appreciated his frank talk of life here at the lake and said yes, she wanted to see the pueblo especially the church we could see in the distance in the plaza. Tacho smiled and said, "We are very proud of our church named Santa Catarina de Palopó, and we have done a lot of work since the quake, but you will see it is not over with. My son Maximiano can accompany you down the trail and introduce you to anyone you may encounter as our friends and that you have talked to me. You can imagine, everyone is suspicious of outsiders."

He whistled, and soon his son, a strapping boy of perhaps 15 arrived, a carbon copy of his father. He was shy but smiled and said it would be his pleasure to guide us. We asked for a short break of about 15 minutes to just sit and contemplate the lake, and we took pictures, and then it was off down the trail to the village, moving very slowly and carefully. I waved goodbye to Tacho after offering him a 20-quetzal bill saying, "Maybe this will help with the harvest. Consider it a gift from one farmer to another."

He accepted it, a bit reluctantly I think, but we both smiled, and he put it in his shirt pocket, smiling saying, "Un placer, que vayan bien en su viaje. Contaré a los amigos que hoy sí conocí a unos gringos simpáticos.! Ha." ["A pleasure, may your travel go well. I will tell my friends that today, yes, I met some 'gringos simpáticos'! Ha."]

It was very slow going, more so than when we climbed up; it was slippery and easy to end up on your rear end. I had noticed Maximiano was without shoes, and we both had good tennis shoes on, but he was the one who scooted down the trail seemingly without difficulty. It figures. He grew up this way. He didn't say much but just said he would watch out for us and explain to anyone we would run into that we were "friends" of his family.

As we got closer to town the outline of the church and the main plaza became clearer. We did notice that all the buildings and houses had that corrugated tin metal for roofs and were told after the quake of 1976 it was the only roof possible. Dozens of people were in effect crushed by the old clay roof tiles everywhere before 1976 (and it was not just poor people; the rich's homes were now tin roofed as well).

It was interesting the church still had the tile roof. The front was beautiful, freshly whitewashed and painted and with the two lions above the doorway, the blue stuccoed pillars and domes on top. The place was empty, but Maximiano said to go on in; he would stand outside in case of any problems. No priest, ladino or Maya, was present, so we never did figure out what the decoration (?) around the doorway was. The entire pueblo had participated in reconstruction of the façade, replacing and placing new roof tiles (an act of faith in itself?). Inside, you could see the latticework of bare roof beams, quite substantial in themselves and the tiles above them. But the inside was still a shambles, small altars covered, except one which revealed a pantheon of Maya Catholic belief.

We were I guess you could say aghast at the row of images, no one there to name them but we for sure could see that the Virgin Mary was in the center, Jesus on the cross to her left, and we guessed St. Joseph to her right. Others might be additional versions of Santa Catarina de Palopó, Mary or not. It was obvious someone was watching over them, the many vases of lilies in front. If one looked carefully there were three paintings on the main altar behind the images, Jesus on the Cross in the center, and above a small but ornate silver tabernacle.

Amy said she didn't know whether to kneel down and pray or cry; my sentiments exactly. What of course hit us between the eyes was that all the figures were obviously ladino or perhaps Jewish, but the dress of all was that provided by the Maya parishioners. I'm saying that made them all the more holy to us and worthy of at least a genuflection and short prayer. Mary in particular was a "picture image" of Maya ladies in all their finery – the hand woven "rebozo" shawl, the local Maya "huipil" and an abundance of what's the word, "fantasy jewelry" necklaces. One other small image to her right, a bearded man, had a shirt or jacket as well of Maya motif.

This was the first time we had seen the saints dressed in Indian clothing; there probably would be many more times, but we both agreed we never felt before so close to their beliefs. We stayed as long as we could, but Maximiano came, saying the morning was getting on, and he had some other things for us to see. First was the "pila" in the center of the plaza in front of the church, Maximiano saying it was the only source of fresh water in the village, a communal well. He wanted to get us down to the shore and to the homemade canoes and get started for the perhaps 45-minute boat trip back to Panajachel.

But as we were walking toward the lake, back up a winding dirt street in the village we could hear music, and always curious for more, I asked Max what was it? He said the men and boys of the town were practicing for the procession of the patron saint's day to come and he could show us but perhaps only for ten minutes; time was of the essence to get to the lake. There was actually a marimba and saxophone, but neither seemed in tune to the other. And there was one man teetering from "huaro." I noted the straw cowboy hats, all the men and boys in regular shirts, but all in those short, woven pants from Santa Catarina patterns. What I remember most was my beloved marimba, out of tune, and the saxophone, where in hell did it come from? Also out of tune.

Maximiano said we had stayed too long, too risky in the canoe on the lake, so it meant a long walk, back up to the trail to the onion patch and retracing our steps back to Panajachel. That was okay with us; we had rain gear, so he accompanied us back up to the hill where his father was wrapping up his day. I gave Max a 5-quetzal bill for his troubles, a bit more than what he would have charged us for the canoe ride home.

On that long walk back "home" we would experience the female side of the lake economy, the ladies in the process of weaving and with samples for sale. I told Amy I could never keep it all straight, which style from which pueblo; she said she had ways of finding that out, even after the fact, one among them a book on Maya weaving throughout the country. The patterns on the huipiles below are all from Santiago Atitlán I think. I bought the white shirt, quite a prize. The ladies offered to show us more and took us just a little way to where one was weaving. We sat and watched and talked for a while. Back strap weaving, Amy said.

Just before we crossed that log bridge back to Panajachel on the left there was a last scene by the lake: a man repairing his canoe, putting pine pitch on to seal the cracks (not totally convincing to me), ladies washing their hair and clothing in the icy waters of the lake, and an unforgettable scene – two sisters freshly bathed, hair washed, clothes cleaned, both images of their mother. We took pictures and offered them a nice "present" in quetzales, I'm sure quite appreciated.

We had made the decision the previous day to move lodging despite how much we enjoyed the Casa Contenta, fulfilling an agreement with Sr. Widemann in Puerto San José. He had arranged for us to enjoy the hospitality of the family inn, El Rancho Grande owned and managed by his niece, Marlita, the daughter of the Widemann brother who had started El Rancho Grande. She was delightful, I think in part because of her uncle's request (I'm sure he clued her in to Amy and her canvasing potential lodging for AT people), but just a good person. The thatched roof (Marlita told us they pay by the strand, and it is really very expensive) and "casitas" were delightful. We settled in, had a drink with her on one of the varandas and had great conversation about the Lake, Panajachel and Guatemala.

There was one down note: it turns out her father, by the way, an old fishing buddy of Señor Meier, Val's dad, was drowned in the lake just two years ago, a victim of the "Xocomil." Marlita just said, "They stayed out fishing too long." We expressed our condolences and she seemed fine but warned to NEVER trust the lake in the p.m. It was a good thing we had walked back to Panajachel and not had that canoe ride with Maximiano (in retrospect, he indeed did know best). We did not discuss the "violencia" of past years, but she simply said things had been rough, especially for the indigenous locals, and that she more than once had been "invited" to host government soldiers at the Rancho. "But things are better now; there is a festival of a saint's day tomorrow in the village so don't miss it, a real slice of life here." We planned for tonight with her at Rancho Grande and tomorrow night a return to the Casa Contenta, just one more day in this magnificent place. Marlita said, "If you want something quite different from the Casa Contenta dining room, a change of pace, I can recommend a small local place with a delightful owner, 'El Cisne.' It is modest, the prices are ridiculously low, the food tasty and with a lot of local color." It was just walking distance from El Rancho down toward the lake, so we decided to go for it. Before that, there was a downpour, and we spent the rest of that afternoon under the veranda of our own casita at El

Rancho, doing the notes for the trip, making some decisions, and planning for tomorrow. Marlita understood that we wanted to spend our last night for nostalgia reasons back at Casa Contenta and dinner and dancing in the lodge. A reprise of a few days ago we hoped!

There are always notes to be added; here is one. We saw an Indian man "cutting" the lawn of El Rancho with a machete!

The photo below is in the kitchen of "El Cisne" with Basilio the owner, his wife, young daughter, and son and another Indian lady, along with the family parakeet. There was no real opportunity to talk in depth, but after a meal costing 2 quetzales each – "sopa, carne asada, legumbres, chile relleno, postre y café" – and a generous tip, we returned to our casita to prepare for the last day at Atitlán.

The next morning there was a portend of rain, so we walked down to the lake early, enjoying the view once again. Afterward we would spend two hours up above in the pueblo for what I think was the annual saint's day celebration; it turned out to be Santa Catarina de Palopó, the same images we saw! And it was memorable.

I'm including two photos, the best up to this point of any indigenous festival we had seen in Guatemala. I don't have too much to say about it but will just describe the things we noted most.

The procession was led by a man with a drum, another with a native flute at his side. We could only surmise the four men behind them were representing the town council of Panajachel itself; they were for sure not part of the indigenous group.

Behind them were two Maya ladies carrying lit incense bowls, then the main saints of the festival came on wooden stands carried by men of the "cofradia" [religious brotherhood], a closer photo to come. This was the patron saint's day, so it was quite an affair, but we learned later from guide Rodolfo that in most of the small indigenous pueblos of Guatemala it is a common custom at least once a week to gather at the house where the saints are kept (not the church, but in the building of the "cofradia" or Maya brotherhood), gather the shamen and others, and "tomarles de paseo" ["take the saints for a walk!"]. It is a hilarious turn of phrase for those of us not Guatemalan or not Maya, but a very serious affair for the natives.

We followed the procession to the "downtown" or main street of Panajachel and caught the following scenes. I believe the image once again is of the Queen of Heaven, the Virgin Mary. Her rebozo and that of the Maya incense lady confirmed what we had seen in Santa Catarina Palopó. The rough, obviously homemade wooden carrier for the image is clearer now.

This next is the best image I could get with my slide camera, not perfect by any means. It seems likely the music is from the group we saw practicing in the pueblo, one can see the marimba in front, a man playing a clarinet to the back left of the marimba, another with a saxophone o his left. The images are guesswork; Amy thinks the Virgin is on the right, perhaps St. Francis in the center and Jesus on the left. Even though it was all very solemn there were one or two men drunk on "huaro" to the side of the group.

Our best picture, in this one St. Francis is on the left, then Jesus, then perhaps St. Joseph and the Virgin to the far right. When I mentioned "huaro," I was thinking of the man in the orangish shirt to the right. The ladies are splendid in their full – length "vestidos" and or "huipiles." The man in the forefront left carries the symbol of the "cofradia." What can I say? There is no professor's lecture, neither Amy nor I knew enough to say other than what we saw, but it was the feeling. We followed the entire procession route and, in some ways, felt like we had done it ourselves. It was beautiful and humble, the poverty of the Indians was visible, but their devotion intact. Taking into consideration all we now knew about Guatemala, it was a good moment.

That evening was glorious – a return to the huge dining hall and salon of the Casa Contenta, a wonderful meal, dancing to the marimba music and private time in our room. Over a night cap we reviewed these few days at el Lago de Atitlán, all we had seen and observed and made notes for James Morrison at AT on what we would recommend for the upcoming trip. We both agreed that Guatemala was not a cut and dried situation; there were definitely pros and cons, but it offered an experience combining ravishing natural beauty with Maya culture that could not be matched.

We were in touch with Rodolfo from AT in Guatemala City, and it was arranged for him to be at the lake at 8 a.m. the next morning, we would have coffee and he would drive us to another highlight of this country, the town of Chichicastenango famous for its market and syncretism of Catholic and Maya religion. After the drive up the steep road to Sololá and the exit to the Pan American Highway, Rodolfo snapped this photo of the two lovebirds. Even though cloudy in this the rainy season, it captures the moment.

# 8

## THE MAYA WORLD OF CHICHICASTENANGO

Rodolfo was driving and pointing out the sights as we climbed eventually to an altitude of about 7000 feet, two thousand more than the lake. There was a continuous stream of Mayas walking, on horses or burros, and some in the back of pickup trucks. More were in those famous multi-colored country buses, many rattletraps, and all belching smoke, all heading to our destination for today is market day. The bummer is it looks like heavy rain coming in. We have reservations tonight at the Maya Inn before heading back to Guatemala City in two days. It is a short stay, but Rodolfo says we can capture the essence of this important modern Maya town in Guatemala.

The first thing that struck me was the agriculture along the way, beautiful manicured "milpas" up the steep hills reminded me of the same back in 1962 on the bus in the Mesilla, from el Tapón to Quetzaltenango, the area and ride I wrote about in "Coming of Age with the Jesuits." One hears about the famous Inca terraces in the Andes, and duly said for they are in arid high mountains and represent an engineering feat to line the terraces with rocks. Amy has been to Machu Picchu but I haven't (that's another story she chides me bout; I did a train ride and an Indian market instead). But these terraces all done by hand labor with those huge hoes I talked about, are indeed impressive. The downside, if there is one, is that for wood and food the forests are being cut down.

We had done some research on this major Maya attraction in Guatemala. The town like many other places received its name from the "Náhuatl" name used by the Indian mercenaries from Tlaxcala Pedro de Alvarado brought with him from Mexico, "Tzitzicaztenanco" converted later to the common "Chichicastenango." It is the municipal seat of the Department of El Quiché, and 95 per cent of its population is Quiché Maya. The majority speak Quiché and Spanish, a small fraction Quiché only, and the rest, Spanish only. It is a major Maya cultural center.

Market is twice a week, and we are here for one of those days. It has rained heavily but Amy and I have good rain gear and can keep our cameras dry. There are many reasons we wanted to come here, the market and all the articles it sells, not just to tourists, but the Mayas themselves, the people and how they pass the day, and of special significance, the "sincretismo" or syncretism of Maya religious rites with Roman Catholicism, famous in these parts.

The altitude is close to 7000 feet and the rain makes it very cool. The Maya Inn where we are lodging has a huge fireplace in the lobby and a rip-roaring fire with lots of people huddled around. The room is small, old, but with lots of wooden beams, and Maya blankets and tapestries cover the room. I'm hoping there is plenty of hot water! We are in no hurry, Rodolfo will meet us the day after tomorrow a.m. at the Inn which turns out to be, incidentally the only realistic upscale place to check out for AT travelers.

We had a full Guatemalan breakfast, some terrific coffee (Mike still limited to one cup) and then figured out a plan of sorts for the next two days: a perusal of the market, and a serious visit to the main religious attraction the Iglesia de Santo Tomás de Chichicastenango.

One immediate item struck me: the smell in the air. If you step outside any door there is a very distinctive smell – the smoke from all manner of fires in the town, most from residences (wood the only source of heat), but a significant amount from the small cooking stoves everywhere in the market, and for the incense that burns everywhere. The second smell – the air seems moldy with all the wetness and no real chance to dry out. All the Indians' clothing seems soaked including the "huipiles, jaquetas, faldas" and such. We had a gringo accoutrement – Gore-Tex rain jackets and pants, and umbrellas. I know we stood out like foreigners, but the price is worth it, no discomfort or colds.

So after that late breakfast it was just a matter of three short blocks to the beginning of the market (we were warned about pickpockets), but the wait to see it all was worth it. Amy and I had seen wonderful indigenous markets in Mexico, especially the one at Oaxaca, but it was inside a huge pavilion. This market was outside, pardon me, more primitive in aspect, but also quite real – the market was indeed for tourists that show up, but it mainly was for the Mayas themselves. The downside today is it has rained, and water stands everywhere, and there is lots of mud, but as the Brits say, you "press on."

Each market stall is as interesting as the next; just a few of the items I remember are food, beans, squash and corn grilled on a charcoal grill, copal incense burners, large "metates" made of limestone for grinding corn to make tortillas. What else? Stands with a myriad of masks which I had to find out about by talking in halting Spanish with the vendor, all kinds of tools (hammers, saws, and especially machetes – I recalled the lawn cutter in Panajachel!) On one street leading out of the market there is the livestock for sale, along with the noise and the smell – pigs, chickens, and even rabbits.

But, pardon my French, the "piéce de résistance" (Amy who actually knows the language heehawed at this turn of phrase from the guy from Nebraska) was Chichi's (pardon again; those who have read my books know I actually hate the use of the common abbreviations; they are demeaning. Examples like L.A., B.A. I hope I will be pardoned because the abbreviation is what the natives use, otherwise a long, long name.) – the weavings and textiles, all native produced throughout the highlands, and most on back looms. Nothing snuck in from Japan or China. It is absolutely mind boggling to see the variety of "huipiles, jaquetas, faldas, pantalones, rebozos" and such. I knew I would never keep it straight but did make sure I got it all in photos. Amy would fill all this in later in Guatemala City where we visited the most famous textile shop – museum in the country. We would use the rest of the afternoon to walk the entire market and around town. Tomorrow would be saved for the church itself and what we hoped would be good scenes of that syncretism I talk so much about.

The standard snack or treat is the corn on the cob, Maya style:

Amy and I sat on the steps of the Church of Santo Tomás and just tried to blend in, for almost two hours, and I got some of the most candid shots ever taken in university and AT travels:

Lunch time for "bebé" as well. Note this huipil! Different!

Even young Maya girls can dream. This photo strikes the heart.

We had sat on those same steps of the Iglesia de Santo Tomás, and after initial nervousness, I got all these candid shots. This is precisely what AT would want for their travelers, but perhaps "coached" to bring the small cameras, be discreet, be patient, be respectful. We were stared at, but it helped to chat a bit in Spanish. It would be back to the Maya Inn for writing pages and pages of notes of what we had seen (and hoped to get home safely on film). Tomorrow promises a very different day – religious syncretism in Chichicastenango. Amy reminded me of the "faux pax" of mine in San Juan Chamula in Mexico researching that trip, so a little discretion was advised.

Our room actually had a small fireplace, and we enjoyed that amenity along with a bottle or two of nice wine while preparing for the next day. There was even time for a bit of intimacy. I hate to use the term, but it was a bit like Amy and I were old marrieds, even though we were not. We had known each other now for so long, had close times before, and even though a wedding was called off, we were very compatible and knew each other well, for better or for worse. Neither of us broached a "what" or "when" after the trip. It was "business" (and fun) as usual. Not a whole lot to update from what I've already reported. The pros and cons of Guatemala were reviewed so far (a beautiful country, a beautiful native Maya people and heritage, historic importance of Antigua, uniqueness of Puerto San José and absolute enchantment with el Lago de Atitlán, BUT, immense poverty, an atmosphere of fear of the military and para – military in the "battle against Communism," little of relative interest in Guatemala City).

The next morning after the now usual "desayuno guatemalteco" of fried eggs, tortillas, black beans, juice and coffee, we had cameras with charged batteries, plenty of film, notepads and ink pens ready, and cool weather and rain gear. It was just a short walk to the church, rainy, muddy and cool again.

I have to admit it was a bit unnerving to see all the huge metal posts supporting the walls hit hard by the earthquake, but it did not seem to bother the locals, crowded on those steps a day earlier for the market and today an amazing scene I will try to describe.

We were getting ready to walk up those church steps and go in when we were interrupted by what I believe is a major scene: the arrival of all the men from the "cofradia" or brotherhood that manages the fiscal matters of the church, the "Cofradía de Pascual Abaj." Dressed identically in black jackets and pants and with a woven headdress we would learn later that is famous for identifying the "cofradia," called a "tzsut" (one could joke I supposed about these guys being the local version of the "suits," ha ha), and the silver staffs with a round medallion with a crucifix on top, an emblem of their status and power!

They marched into the church, gathered in front at the altar with the local Catholic priest, said what seemed a litany of prayers but in Quiché Maya and promptly marched out. We witnessed the whole thing seated in hard wooden pews but remained just watching and waiting. Unlike San Juan Chamula in Chiapas, Mexico, a few years ago, light was streaming into the church, at least enough to make out the bare, very poor inside, and I was able to take a picture (no flash of course) without any consequences. The latter I think because this church is so famous and is on the regular tourist route and everyone is used to the hubbub.

We sat quiet and respectfully for about thirty minutes, distracted by the constant coming and going of tourists, all wielding cameras, large and small. I do not have an accurate report of what we saw, but there was a Maya lady in full dress of "huipil y falda" and a man to her side in "ladino" clothing, both with many candles lit and flower petals surrounding them. I can only surmise these were prayers and offerings. The scene was very different from San Juan Chamula with the glass boxes of saints and armed guards with clubs. This was a relief I guess from what we went through in Mexico, but maybe not quite so exciting.

What I can report here is the general information given to us in a brochure at the Maya Inn: The church is 400 years old (it looks it), and like so many Catholic churches it was built following the custom of the "conquistadores" on top of an old Maya temple. Incidentally, for those Anglos who find this repulsive, it is. But one should know that in the classic Maya culture and times the same thing happened: when one king died, the next reduced his temple to rubble and built a new one on top of it, commemorated of course to himself. We saw the candles and smelled the burning incense, both noted for prayers of the shamen of today. I had not noticed, but there are 18 steps up to the church entrance; they say these reflect the 18 months of the Maya calendar year.

One final note. After leaving the church and heading back to the Maya Inn to meet Rodolfo, there was yet one major purchase. I bought an actual "tzsut" or woven headdress from the lady pictured below. It was expensive but incredibly fine weaving and most of all, an accurate "recuerdo" of what we had just seen.

There seemed to be no shortage of the article, so I can only assume others made a similar purchase. Once again, the complexity of all the Maya weaving, patterns, from which village or ethnic group escapes me, but we did find a real jewel of a book at that textile shop in Guatemala City which illuminates it all, "The Highland Maya."

So, it was an incredibly memorable morning, I close this segment of the trip with this photo.

The scene of one of the members of the Cofradía with the "Ttsut."

# 10

# RESPITE AND PLANNING
# IN GUATEMALA CITY

Rodolfo picked us up after a last "café con leche" at the Inn and we began the drive back to Guatemala City. I digress, but we would see an incredibly sad sight then and in days to come, market days to towns in the highlands. There would be Indigenous men passed out on the sides of the road, often with their wives patiently sitting beside them waiting I guess for them to sleep it off. We saw one such memorable scene that day after leaving the market at Chichicastenango.

There was the now "obligatory" stop at Katok for sausages and tortillas for most folks, something less for me, but then the short detour promised by Rodolfo days earlier to Iximché. I had been to the site and to boot via horseback from the "finca" from friend Val Meier's back in 1962. Amy and I recalled from the history lessons in Antigua how important it was and is at least symbolically yet today.

From 1470 to 1547 it was the capital of the Kakquichel kingdom who had at one time been allies of the Quiché, both peoples originally lived in the Quiché capital of Utatlán. They later became enemies and the Kakquicheles founded their own center of Iximché. It is complicated and strange. The Aztecs when invaded and defeated by the Spaniards in Tenochtitlán in 1521 sent word to the Kakquicheles and warned them, so the latter actually sent envoys to the Spaniards offering to be their allies in Guatemala under the Conquistador Pedro de Alvarado. They helped in subduing other Maya groups in the highlands including the Quiché and in 1524 Iximché was named the first capital of Guatemala under the Spaniards. There was soon a falling out because of high taxes and labor demands from the Spaniards, then conflict and final surrender in 1530. It did not help the Kakquicheles that they had been decimated by smallpox even before the arrival of Alvarado.

We were returning to Guatemala City via the main highway now, the Pan American Highway and it was a clear day, so we saw the beautiful valley the city is located it and the Volcán de Fuego spewing smoke in the distance. We settled in once again at the Hilton, visited Amy's French restaurant that night and began making plans for the major trip north to the lowlands of the Petén and the amazing pre - Columbian Maya site of Tikal, near the top of our list for this trip.

But there was one small but very significant happening the next day, courtesy of a history professor at the National University of San Carlos, we saw the original manuscript of Bernal Díaz del Castillo, "La Verdadera Historia de la Conquista de México" ["The True Story of the Conquest of Mexico"], one of the most significant tomes ever written about those days. The author's claim to fame was that his was the story of a simple, unlettered soldier and combatant from the beginning of Spanish ventures from the Dominican Republic to the Yucatán to Tenochtitlán. Bernal Díaz died in Guatemala in 1584 after spending his final years as an alderman in Santiago de los Caballeros (the old capital near Antigua) and the book was not published until 1632. The story is so convoluted with so many ups and downs and twists and turns, I can't repeat it here. Suffice to say he battled courts, the crown, other conquistadores, and assorted bureaucrats for years to get and protect the land grants supposedly given him for his role in Mexico and then Guatemala. And the story would make your hair curl. The manuscript bound in leather that we saw seemed legitimate enough, but it is all contested. We both agreed that this was a valuable moment, if for nothing else than understanding how complicated life could be in those days.

# 11

## ADVENTURE RESEARCH TRAVEL TO TIKAL

So the next morning we were off on an old dependable (?) DC -3 airplane from Aviateca the National Airlines of Guatemala from Guatemala City to an infinitesimally small gravel landing strip outside of Tikal. Before I tell of our time at that incredible place, a bit of history and yes, archeology.

There are several theories where the name "Tikal" comes from, but I like best the one from the Maya Itzá Tradition – "The Place of the Voices." (We shall hear them.) It is listed as 188 miles north of Guatemala City, but as the crow flies, it is about the same to the east of the magnificent site Amy and I saw in Mexico at Palenque, all classic Maya sites.

Tikal was a jewel of the Classic Period from approximately 300 to 900 A.D. It is located in thick tropical rain forest (both an advantage and disadvantage to be seen) in the Department of the Petén in the northern Guatemala lowlands and is close to other important sites like Yaxchilán and Uaxactún. Rivals from its age were Calakmul to the northwest and Caracol in Belize. In my days of study before this trip with Amy, and I mainly pushing AT so hard for a possible expedition, I discovered the site was sometimes used in an analogy as the "New York" of the Mayas referring to the immense height of several of its pyramid – temples (as opposed to the "Paris" of the Mayas at Copán in Honduras for the complexity and art of its carved stelae). It is also located in a national park (since 1955) and much of the pleasure of the site is found in experiencing the tropical forest, the animals such as Howler Monkeys, immense flocks of parrots and even the cutter ants at work in the forest. The site is large, some six square miles. It was discovered in 1848, rediscovered in 1877 and again in 1904.

They estimate there are 3000 structures in Tikal. Several of the major edifices including the tall pyramids (five when Amy and I are there) are excavated, but many small ones not. All are built on limestone shelves with many cisterns to their side paved in clay for water preservation in the dry season. Causeways or cobbled roads connected the different sectors of the "city." Because of the immensity of the site yet to be excavated, there is a major problem. Just an aside, Amy and I were informed that at the present time we are headed to Tikal that tomb robbers are still active, at night to be sure, but, well, it is a warning.

The area was populated as early as 600 B.C., but Tikal came into its own between the 6th and 9th centuries A.D. Once thought of as a city of "peaceful philosophers" by early scholars of the Maya, it is now known more accurately because of the successful deciphering of the hundreds of Mayan glyphs on its stelae (to come). They indicate that the dynasty of kings of Tikal ruled in despotic fashion and was in fact in fierce competition for territorial expansion with neighboring city – states such as Calakmul and later on Quiriguá. There is now confirmed evidence of war, bloodshed, capture of enemy soldiers and to some extent human sacrifice, thus contradicting the "really romantic views" of the early scholars (Sylvanus Morley the pioneering writer most quoted).

Notwithstanding the above, Maya accomplishments in tropical agriculture, conservation of water, the art of sculpting its historical markers, the stelae, and the painting of ceramics with the same "glyph markers," and perhaps most importantly, the monumental construction of its temples are to be reckoned with. The Mayan language in effect made it possible for them to write history on stone and ceramics. And the interest in astronomy and the long – count in Mathematics allowed them to achieve knowledge and greatness. The pantheon of Mayan spirits and gods is a story in itself. The important historic link between the leaders of early Tikal and the magnificent civilization of Teotihuacán in central Mexico marks an important part of their history and early development.

Back to the airplane. We were both a bit taken aback by the DC-3 on the small landing strip across the airport from the international jets, jet props and Guatemalan Air Force Planes, the latter what the locals call the "real" airport in Guatemala City. Someone somewhere once compared this plane to an old, tired, lazy hound dog back on its haunches. This is our jalopy of transportation to the landing strip in the forest surrounding Tikal. As mentioned, it is a DC-3 of Aviateca Airlines of Guatemala, but for me a throwback to the same I flew in at various times in the Amazon of Brazil and the interior of the Northeast during doctorate study days. Still an amazingly reliable airplane, its main virtue is it can land on the miniscule airstrip carved from the forest at Tikal, at least most of the time. There is perhaps a minor point: one went down in a rainstorm when it was hit by lightning last week. They assure us of good weather. I'm thinking another "adventure in flight!" Ha!

You climb a small, metal ladder up into the plane at a small door behind the wing. That explains the short, metal ladder. The old seats are big, fat stuffy affairs that remind me of old cars from the 1940s in the U.S., but there are two stewards and one stewardess in spiffy airline uniforms. We are served a nifty light breakfast of orange juice, wonderful "café con leche" and the best sweet rolls yet in Guatemala. The flight is to be two hours at turtle speed, about 100 air miles per hour. I cannot tell you how thrilled and excited we both are to see Tikal - the major reason we are in Guatemala – home of the classic Maya. I wrote later:

We were flying so low that you could clearly see the mountains of the highlands, towns below and then the gradual entry into the lowlands and the Guatemalan rain forest where the Mayas founded and lived their greatest moments. This alone was serendipitous. The low altitude plus a bit of an adventurous Latino pilot who decided to fly us around the ruins twice before landing (or before he got any instructions or clearance that there were no animals on the airstrip) made for the next two photos I took from the plane. They are among the most exciting of all my years of study and the trips with Amy for AT, a bit distant and then a close-up view of the entire site of Tikal.

It is difficult to describe, but perhaps the reader will understand. In spite of travel on an airplane and that sector of the wing we can see, that view made me think that THIS is exactly as it was a little over one thousand years ago.

The rest of the flight on that early morning turned out to be uneventful, well, maybe not. It was white knuckle all the way when our Guatemalan "Top Gun" literally dropped us from the tops of low trees onto that clay runway, hit his air brakes and slowly rolled to a stop about 15 yards from the trees at the other end. He had to do a tight maneuver to just turn the plane around and then taxi to the "terminal." The less than perfect air conditioning or at least air – moving fans in the plane were turned off, we waited nervously for some fresh air and got it, sort of, when they finally opened the single door down to that metal ladder to the ground. There's a cliché - the humidity and heat after Atitlán and Chichicastenango hit us like a ton of bricks. I looked at Amy, she smiled weakly and did that shrugging gesture of hands with her palms up. Soooo?

The "terminal" was a small, one room shack with a couple of old radio antennae on top. We had to wait in line in the sun while each of us confirmed the return flight to Guatemala City, and that sunshine did not help temperaments. Fortunately, the agent was efficient with the paperwork. We were not allowed in, but I assume there was radio equipment inside. Luggage (and we had been limited to one small bag each plus pack and or camera equipment) was transferred to the back of an old blue school bus and we were boarded fairly quickly. The bus did have several fans turning so no one passed out. They had bottles of cold (but not icy) water from a cooler as you got on. DC - 3's do not hold many passengers, and that's a good thing because we all fit well into the bus. The ride that followed took just a few minutes.

The blue bus took us to our lodging, the famous (or infamous) "Posada de la Selva" ["Jungle Lodge"]. As an introduction I'll just say the name was indeed apropos.

We were driven on a well-maintained road through the forest clearings. Off to the side there were green mounds, some with small trees on them. The driver – guide announced that these were unexcavated small temples.

Our destination was the Great Plaza, but we first stopped with a view of Complex Q which turned out to be a prototype of many (9 in all): two small temples facing each other, each with stelae in front, and altars. Our first stelae, maya arch and glyphs!

The Maya arch is "not considered a true arch" by sniffy archeologists wanting to compare it to the rounded arch of Arabia, then Rome and Europe of "more advanced" civilizations or cultures. But it still bears commentary: stones on each side, each slightly wider vertically above the one below, on a slant; both sides higher until the arch is completed with a wide rectangular capstone above. The physics works: such an arch will support heavy walls. The problem is it does not allow for large interior rooms; the Mayas solved this at Palenque in Mexico using double arches to support more weight, thus constructing that famous stairway Amy and I saw in the Palace of the Inscriptions (and where we had that "scrape" with a Náhuatl nationalist, read the book, huh?). We noted there was no roof or ceiling in the complex building, this because they had original thatch roofs.

The complexes were believed to be built each 20 years or "Katun" in the Maya calendar. We were disappointed with these stelae because they had either no or worn carving. We were informed they were 1300 years old, weathered, but to be patient, to hold our architectural horses, as we would say in Nebraska.

After the two small complexes, we drove behind one of the two main acropolises of the Great Plaza, and the driver noted a small, dark doorway leading to a black tunnel, saying this was current excavation and many new finds are taking place. Then in short order the blue bus parked, and we all got out at the side of Temple II. We presumed we would be on our own the rest of the day before drinks and dinner at the "Posada de la Selva."

Amy and I then walked through a narrow passage to the side of Temple II to the "Plaza Mayor" and its open view and grandeur. We gasped at the sight and were basically struck silent by what we saw: Temple II in front of us and partially excavated Temples III and IV in the forest beyond.

If that were not enough, across the plaza was the "Templo del Juguar Gigante" ["Temple of the Gigantic Jaguar"] or Temple I, in all its grandeur:

It is difficult to describe a place so dreamed about and yet it still surpassed the dream. As we stood just taking it all in, a swarthy, dark-complected Guatemalan approached us, tipped his hat, and introduced himself. "Yo soy Inspector de Policía de Tikal, Teniente Javier Kax. It is my pleasure to welcome you to Tikal; our agents in Guatemala City informed us you were coming, and we saw your names on the flight manifesto. I assume you are Profesor Michael Gaherty y Señorita Amy Carrier of Adventure Travel. I have been assigned to accompany you to see the marvels of Tikal and also to assure your safety." After a very short chat, we tried to gently inform Office Kax (a famous Maya name I'll talk of later), we would prefer to see the Plaza ourselves since we had a list of planned items to check out (trying not to offend him or get on his wrong side) but would he like to have a drink with us at the Posada and then join us for lunch? He seemed to perk up at that, saying he recognized our need for privacy but he or his men would be keeping an eye on us.

I'll try not to overwhelm the reader with details, but the general layout of the Plaza is like this: to one end is the tallest pyramid, Temple I or the "Templo del Jaguar Gigante," to the other the slightly less tall Pyramid II, but wider. But to either side in the middle are the "acropoli" or series of buildings and/or temples with a row of carved stelae in front. The Acropolis del Norte is on one side (the Temple I doorway on top faces east) and the Acropolis Central to the other.

In an indented doorway of the Central Acropolis there is a surprise -a large carved stone mask of Tlaloc – the rain god of Teotihuacán in central Mexico. Just as in Kaminaljuyu, the less than impressive (to me) pre – classic site on the outskirts of Guatemala City, here the Teotihuacano influence is significant. The scientists explain that in the very early days of Tikal there indeed was a Teotihuacán priest – chieftain who would be influential in the formation of what would become one of the grandest cities of the Mayas! One could climb down into the opening in the temple to see this image which has the traits of Teotihuacán but surprisingly (to us anyway) was covered by a simple sheet of corrugated tin to keep off the rain and sun. I'm no expert but the large ear plugs were the first sign of Teotihuacán.

We spent the next two hours seeing all the stelae in the Plaza and documenting each one with both of our cameras. Some of them I recognized from books studied before in graduate school or more recently "National Geographic Magazine." Remember, Amy and I had seen the carved images at Palenque (not free-standing stelae but carvings on stone or stucco on the walls, but with the largest Maya text known in the interior of the Temple of the Inscriptions). So, I guess a short primer is in order for the stelae.

The stelae vary from one classic – era site to another, these at Tikal are important but are just among many in the entire classic area (Copán in Honduras is coming up if all goes well). We know today because of the work of Mayanist Linda Schele of the University of Texas and David Stuart that these stone monoliths are really markers of Maya history. They vary from two to perhaps five meters in height, are about one yard square, two sides generally depicting Maya figures, two sides with glyphs explaining each stone and its purpose. They are representations of nobles – priests – warriors – masculine kings – feminine spouses with carved scepters in hand, jade earrings, nose plugs, breast plates, wide belts, all highly ornate and carved in the stones. The stones of Tikal are six to seven feet tall. There is generally one carved figure on one side, but perhaps another on the opposite. On the lateral sides there is often, not always, a Mayan text, squares with glyphs carved in stone. On the belts and breastplates of many are depicted images of Mayan spirits and gods.

As mentioned, about 90 per cent of the Mayan glyphs now have been deciphered or "read." There is an immense literature dealing with this, from the early book by Morley, to the latest by Schele, Stuart, Michael Coe and colleagues. What Morley thought were glyphs telling only of numbers and dates, we now know were telling much more, in effect, the "story" of the figures depicted upon the stelae, in effect, historical markers. It was Linda Schele who emphasized that Maya "history" begins with these stone monuments, a carved history to be sure. The Maya language (and its many variants) as seen in its glyphs would evolve, grow, and one day be forgotten.

The famous Maya "books" are a whole other story: glyphs and illustrations on a rough paper or bark surface. Only three are left in the world, in Madrid, Paris and Dresden, this after a "book-burning" by Bishop Landa in the Yucatán believing the texts were contrary to his "Católicismo" and even works of the devil!

I just add now that the ceramics of Tikal and classic Maya sites use glyphs as well. I've included two photos, never enough, to give a good idea of what Amy and I saw.

We were soaking with sweat, tired, thirsty in spite of warm bottled water, so were ready for the walk to the Posada. We had just scratched the surface of what Tikal had to offer. Hungry and maybe ready for a nap before Tikal, "Part II." I haven't said much about the "Posada de la Selva," but no time like the present for an, ahem, notable stay.

There were really several buildings: a huge central "long house" with the restaurant, "dormitory" style lodging, and small private "casitas" for couples who craved a bit more privacy. More on that later. The restaurant took up perhaps one half of the long house; it had that huge, thatched roof you can see in the photo but with wooden beams below, long rows of simple tables with tablecloths and wooden chairs. It was all rather spartan, and even rough. I might add one could stay in the large city of Flores, capital of the Petén region, several hours by bus or jeep from the site and with "modern" hotels, but both Rodolfo and Nataniel of AT said for the authentic "jungle" experience the Posada was the choice. We both had showers before the "almuerzo." More on our "room" later but suffice to say it was small with two beds, a wooden table with a lamp, and walls only about three feet high, on top of that was what we used to call in Nebraska as "chicken wire." So much for privacy, but everyone seemed willing to trade that for a "real jungle experience!" Ha! Men's and women's privies were down the way with unspeakable sanitation conditions, a cold-water spigot for the shower and bring your own soap. We cleaned up, and even the amazingly cool water felt good.

Teniente Javier was waiting for us at the door of the dining room, a big smile on his face with those perfect white teeth the natives have, some say from the "maíz" tortillas in their diet. We sat opposite each other at one of the long, unpretentious dining tables. We had cold bottled water and a Gallo national beer for me. Javier wondered how we found Tikal thus far, and Amy and I gushed in our enthusiasm. He was amazed we both knew so much about Tikal but when I explained I studied it all in college and even taught about it, he smiled again, congratulating us on being "informed tourists." We ordered the "menú del día," the only option: rice, beans, tortillas and grilled chicken, all very tasty. (Amy and I laughed when the same "menu" was offered later that evening.)

After explaining a bit who we were, why we were here and our aspirations for sights to see for a possible AT trip, we got around to talking about him. Kax is an old Maya name, in fact, famous, meaning "corn" so what more appropriate? Yum Kax is the Maya corn god! Javier was born in a tiny Maya village just 10 kilometers from the park, one of seven children. He grew up speaking Maya and only learned Spanish in the school reached by bus two hours away. He explained there were really no opportunities for a "career" but only work in a logging operation nearby (there used to be hardwoods in the Petén but they are being harvested and sold mainly to Japan and the U.S.), so he joined the Guatemalan army. Ironically, they wanted someone who could speak Maya dialects and Spanish, so he was needed and used to translate in villages all over the highlands but also in the Petén. I took a big breath and asked, "But what about 'la violencia' and the stories we had been hearing of genocide against the natives?"

He grew silent, pondering his answer, and said, "I did see some horrible things, but I also saved many lives. There were times I would tell the commanders that the particular village we were entering had no link at all to the 'guerrilleros,' and the locals had no contact with them, so we should move on. In the last three years I was able to be on duty in the Petén and close to Tikal and Uaxactún; the dialect of Maya we speak in my village is different from either Kakchiquel Quiché Maya of the highlands. When I mustered out one year ago, I was fortunate to be offered the security job here in the park; it pays fairly well, enough to support me, my young wife and now two children, and have some left over for our parents.

"We in my village really had little to do with the park itself but were often involved with loggers and even what I suspect were tomb robbers. This year has been one of much study, of learning of the site but also of constant vigilance for evil goings-on. I could tell you many stories. Suffice to say I have survived two shoot outs with the "rateros," killed a few of them, and am valued greatly by the Park Superintendent for my work. Believe me, I would much rather be on duty here at the site, helping people like you, but my colleagues and I are often called for 'emergencias.'"

Amy was squirming by this time. She asked Javier in Spanish, "Is it safe to bring 20 to 30 of our 'Adventurers' to this place?"

"Amy, I can never say 100 per cent, but close to it. If your travelers come in a supervised, organized group, stay at the recommended lodging, utilize the guides and our own park security services and mainly do NOT go out at night, unless in my company or that of one of my officers, all will be okay."

I piped up, "So Javier, maybe we can go out tomorrow night. I want to see the night animals in the park; they say there is a slight chance of a 'tigre' or jaguar."

"Miguel, for sure there are animals at night you would never see during the day. Let's talk tomorrow, see what my schedule and obligations are looking like, okay? Meanwhile I suggest you do the Plaza Mayor Temples, and the walk over to Temples III and IV and the acropolises, that should keep even you busy! Ha ha. After lunch we were ready for a nap, but the heat was too much in spite of the large overhead electric fans in each room. Javier suggested we do the Museum with its air conditioning and start the Temple viewing tomorrow morning. So be it.

# THE MUSEUM OF TIKAL

The museum was small, its main virtue it had air conditioning, not great but better than the outside heat and humidity (Tikal did cool temporarily very early around dawn and for a very short while with dense tropical rains in the p.m. The University of Pennsylvania was the main excavator and had an archeological team at the site for I guess some 50 years; I think they may have taken some good artifacts home to Philadelphia for their troubles. We saw ceramics with wonderful images and glyphs, more stelae, but the treat was the artist painstakingly doing an ink "drawing" for some kind of cloth article.

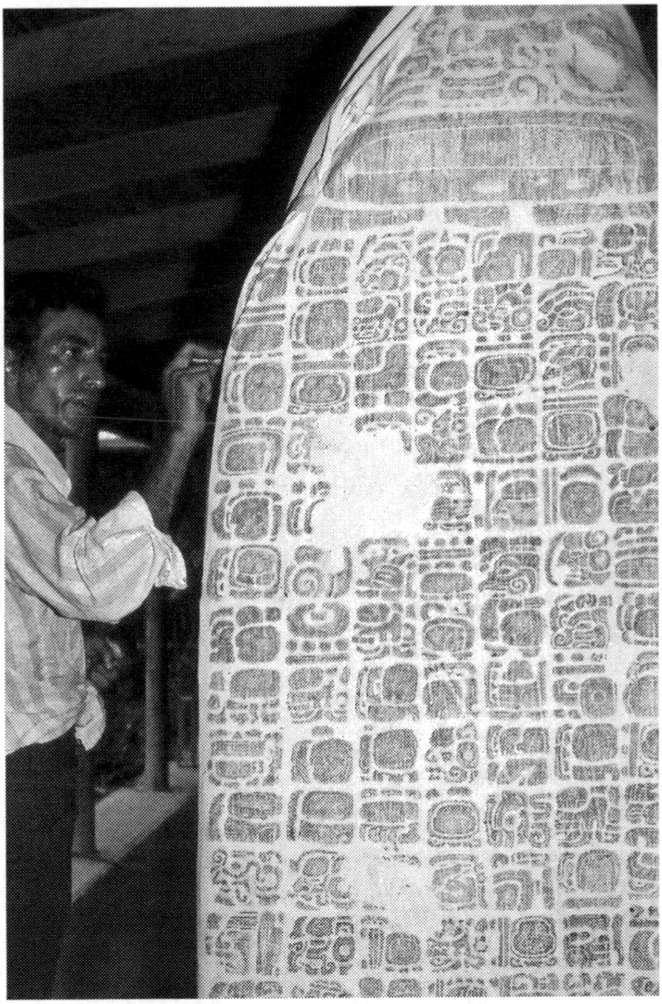

I am anxious to tell the reader about the next huge day visiting the large temples, but have to admit both Amy and I were a bit groggy that a.m. There was a reason, no, wait, there may have been two or three. Entomology for one. (My Mom when I was in high school said there were two good careers for a farm boy – livestock auctioneer and study of bugs and how to eradicate them for crops.) It's worth a paragraph. The Jungle Lodge room had the two small beds, a rough table, a wooden chair. The community bathrooms were outside along a walkway. We drank some beer after dinner talking to other guests, and probably turned out lights at 10 p.m. So sure enough, a bathroom call was in order about 2 a.m. Complications ensued.

It turns out electric power comes from a generator, and it is turned off at around midnight. Each "guest" gets a box of wooden matches and a candle. I put mine on the floor next to my bed. In the pitch dark (that word means something in the jungle) I woke up having to pee, moved around trying to find the matches and after touching for sure what I thought were beetles, found them and the matches. I struck a match. Santa María! There was a loud buzzing sound in the room and we both discovered that the entire floor and wall were covered with insects. I found my tennis shoes, turned them over and knocked out any critters and literally crunched my way to that bathroom. Perhaps a kinky entomologist would have gotten off, but it was just plain scary to me.

Women are supposed to be afraid of mice but add a carpet of bugs to that. Spider Man would have been on tiptoes there! Amy shrieked and I swore. We managed to do our duty and get back to bed. The amazing thing, we did sleep a bit until early dawn. In the morning, no bugs in sight. Hmm? We had one more night to go in that @#$%&& place! A full day of investigating ruins today, one – half day the next morning and the plane back to Guatemala City after lunch. Stay tuned.

# THE HEIGHTS OF TEMPLES AND THE FEAR

After that usual Guatemalan breakfast of eggs, black beans and tortillas and just a bit of coffee, we were into the ruins when the gates opened. Déjà vu all over again? (The reader might recall our climbing the "Castillo" at Chichén – Itzá or the Temple of the Inscriptions in Palenque or the Temple of the Magician in Uxmal a few years ago.) Heights scare the crap out of me, fortunately not Amy. However, there was no way I would not get to the top of Temple I ("El Templo del Jaguar Gigante"), Tikal's tallest excavated, Temple II and later Temple IV. A big order.

It was warming up, but still some coolness in the air at 6:00 a.m. Finally! Temple I! A blurb: constructed around 700 A.D. commemorating the king "Pata de Jaguar" ["Jaguar Paw"], it is 145 feet high (maybe 15 U.S. stories). Above the small temple on top is what they call a roof comb- a carved image of a seated individual in highly ornamental dress, all worn down with time. There is a chain in the middle of the Temple I stairway, the steps are steep (how did the relatively short Maya do this?), worn from thousands of tourists and slippery. Amy went first, scrambling up like one of those famous howler monkeys (yet to be seen) and sat on the floor outside the doorway of the temple at the top. I was much slower, doing what Javier Kax had recommended: hang on, move slowly, face only in front of you, do NOT look to the side or, God forbid, behind you. I reached the top, crawled carefully onto the small platform, put my back against the wall and tried to breathe deeply and calm the nerves, Amy holding on to my arm. In what seemed like a very long time I got the courage to open my eyes and take in this scene:

After that terrifying climb down Temple I, me hanging on for dear life, and a rest and a snack and water, it was time to walk across the plaza to Temple II. Slightly less tall than Temple I, 124 feet high, but wider, the temple is larger and with some surviving artifacts: inside walls are decorated with "grafitos," or drawings done by hand of various Maya symbols, including one of a dead man with a lance through his chest! The carved wooden interior roof beam ("dintel" or "lintel") that was in place is in the Museum of Natural History in NYC. It depicts a figure of a Maya noble, perhaps a woman, dressed ornamentally in a long dress with the large image of Tlaloc, the god of rain at Teotihuacán (more evidence of that connection). The view out its door is incredible: Temple I and the jungle beyond.

Because time was short and still well before lunch hour, we decided to take on the "Acropoli". The North Acropolis was probably begun about 200 B.C. and contains the tombs of the principal rulers of the time. These are buried according to Maya custom; successive new temples were built at the death of each king. Many of the stelae are in the Museum and the lower building houses that carving of Tlaloc. We found the other

"Acropolis," the "Central Acropolis," more interesting. You can see the doorways above. The archeologist Maler lived in one of the rooms while doing initial research on Tikal in 1890. Amy said his clothes would have been a bit moldy and in need of a good wash and ironing. There were "graffitos" as in Temple I, clay floored water reservoirs to the side, water stored from thunderstorms and tropical rain. An aside: as in the Yucatan, the soil of the area is of limestone and water seeps through the thin soil easily; thus the "cisterns."

The several temples in the Central Acropolis had a major maya building secret: the corbeled or "Maya Arch," the most advanced we had seen were in Palenque before in Mexico. As mentioned, this arch is not a true rounded arch as in Roman or Arabic times, but an arch dependent on a "capstone" to support the two walls. I was able to photograph one excellent example in a temple interior room:

One additional point: the Maya ballgame courts. There are three at Tikal, but very small, nothing like the amazing court at Chichén Itzá. There were no tall walls with rings. I repeat what the experts say: "The game was played by three players on each side; they could 'hit' the hard rubber ball with their chest. This explains the few 'proofs' that exist, that players wore a sort of 'pechero' or chest protector, probably of thick cotton." The same experts surmise (?) the ballgame was played to the death with the sacrifice of the losing players, a concept not proved at least in the case of Tikal. Grizzley just the same; the experts tie it all into religion and the forces of nature. An aside: the more Amy and I read of the Maya, the more complicated and confused it became. All those "experts'" words were: "maybe, perhaps, possibly, probably" and the like.

I also won't go deeply into the myriad theories for the demise of the Classic Era (Tikal, Palenque, Bonampak, Copán to name some). Just say some believe it was a prolonged drought with resulting hunger, but recent accounts say there was warfare, loss of many lives, and sites were actually abandoned later.

Hot, sweaty, exhausted but with more that had to be seen today, we stopped, returned to the Posada de la Selva, had showers and the main noon meal once again. Javier Kax was there, a big smile on his face and wanting to know our views. "Terrific, more than meeting expectations." Amy and I did discuss AT and the possible trip to come in view of recent experiences. Would elderly AT adventurers be up to the heat, humidity and rough living at Tikal, i.e. the lodge, the bathrooms, and the bugs? An alternative would be a nice hotel in Flores, the modern capital of the Petén and a several-hour ride distant. We both from now several years' experience knew that most Adventurers travel the world, are tough folks, and would want no less than the true on – site experience. To be seen.

One final foray that p.m. was to go to the partially excavated Pyramid IV, climb to the top with what Javier promised would be a spectacular view, come back, shower and he would give us a special nighttime nature walk of the Park. All right! On the way to Temple IV, we necessarily stopped to see a major artifact:

Seemingly planted in the middle of the trail was famous Altar 5 and Stela 16. The altar has glyphs in a circle all around it as well as the dots and bars indicating the time the work was done, and in the center are two figures. Are they priests, nobles, or warriors? Once again, we surmised the "perhaps, maybe or probably" of experts. Both are in fine classic garb and are kneeling before a skull and bones. The face of the skull is defaced as usual as on most of the stelae and other images of Tikal. The reason for the defacing was never explained convincingly to me, whether vengeance by conquerors or whatever. Modern day archeologists say that the contemporary natives' dislike of tourist cameras may be related: the photo may "capture" their spirit! This altar, say the archeologists, proves the existence of human sacrifice at Tikal! And this in turn brings up a serious long debated subject: the entire question of human sacrifice. An aside is to be permitted:

For many decades in the 20th century, and really from the beginnings of the 19th, the Maya Civilization was thought to be more "civilized" and certainly less blood-thirsty than that of their neighbors the Aztecs in Mexico (or their antecedents at Teotihuacán or Tula in Mexico). Scholars called them the "Greeks of America" and the Aztecs "the Romans." The former was thought of as peace-loving, a nation of "philosopher-priests." They were judged to be beyond the concept of human sacrifice. As time has passed, the glyphs deciphered and more evidence unearthed, literally, it is now accepted that indeed they practiced war, and war of conquest, and that prisoners were taken, and sacrifice took place. In fact, it became known that the greatest sacrifice was the bloodletting of the king himself. The dripping of blood from his penis on sacred "paper" which was subsequently burned produced smoke rising to the heavens. The smoke was understood as prayer or supplication to their gods, and his was the "greatest" sacrifice. There are stelae in the Natural History Museum of Mexico City that show this bloodletting. I mentioned to Amy that I have always found the use of incense in Roman Catholic services to be, ironically, of similar import. Amy said, "Hmmm, never thought of it that way, Gaherty, you should have been an archeologist or at least a grave digger or tomb robber! Ha!" Under any circumstances Altar 5 is magnificent!

And among further amateur speculation, I could only remember this stone with its circle of glyphs being reminiscent of the "Aztec Calendar," not really that but a monument to its evil sun god. Just a whim, not really. Just a coincidence, right? More likely, just a professor's ramblings. More strenuous activity, the climb to Temple IV interrupted the musings.

Others were headed the same way, students I surmised, very tough and slow going, very hot and sweaty, but not like climbing pyramid stairways! It was worth it because up above that p.m. there was a cool breeze and with a view unequaled:

The acropolis can be seen to the left, the main plaza with Temples I and II in the center, Temple III closer to us. Amy and I and a few others just sat at the top of Temple IV, cooled off a bit, but marveled at the grandeur of the scene. This was, indeed, Maya Civilization!

It was late afternoon, after that unforgettable scene that we heard and saw, albeit with an amateur's photo, the famous Howler Monkeys of Tikal. We had seen them before at Palenque in Mexico, but these really gave a show, bouncing around in the trees. This would be another item near the top of the list for our Adventurers.

And on the return to the lodge just moments later we witnessed in all its glory, the phenomenon of the Cutter Ants at work in the jungle. If one looks very carefully, there is a winding, slow moving row of partially cut or whole green leaves. There is an ant below each one, and they were moving slowly but incredibly methodically to one presumes, a hill with the Queen inside waiting to chow down! Neither of us in our travels had seen such a sight.

Amy said, "Enough already, Gaherty, I'm convinced. AT should and must do this." We smiled, glad to agree, and were once again thinking positive about the trip. In twenty minutes more we were back at the Posada, another shower from the humidity, a couple of cold (but not icy) Guatemalan Gallo beers, and time for a rest and supper. Javier had said he would be there after supper, equipped to give us that personal guide to the nature of Tikal that night.

## TIKAL BY NIGHT

"Equipped." Hmm. He had a powerful lantern, a pistol with ammunition belt around his waist, and what looked like an old Winchester 73 rifle next to him. "Just in case, 'no se preocupen.'" Hmmm.

We set off on one of the many organized trails and the first thing you noticed was the noise, or at times, the lack of it. Jaime took us through groves of trees, lianas hanging from them. When he had a "spot," he would shine the powerful flashlight on it – we saw coati mundis sleeping in a treetop, they just looked lazily down at us. There was a rustle on the trail in front of us, and critters I did not recognize raced across, Jaime barely with time for the spot. They were like small tapirs we had both seen in Brazil, the Brazilian "agouti," red or brown with spots along the side. It's a rodent and I might add, a big rodent.

Jaime suddenly stopped, motioned for "hush," and shined his light on some heavy brush to the side where we saw two small yellow eyes staring back at us – shivers down my spine for sure, it was an ocelot, crouching in the brush, not making a move.

We headed deeper into the forest, Jaime saying only he and his men or natives ever were in this area, no tourists ever allowed here. The trail was narrow, the path damp but not muddy, but then it happened: in a small clearing ahead of us Jaime heard a growl and turned the spot on it, "shush." The cat froze in its tracks, evidently surprised at the intrusion. It was indeed a full-grown jaguar (we had seen a magnificent one in the zoo at Las Ventas in Mexico on that scary research trip for AT a few years ago). The animal seemed to be daring us to come closer, flexing muscles in powerful legs. We all froze, waiting, Jaime ever so slowly raising the rifle in his arms. A few minutes later, bored or tired, but evidently fearless, the animal moved off into the underbrush. Jaime was excited, telling us indeed he had seen only a handful his entire life and indeed we are blessed!

Can we ever be satisfied? Amy and I both lamented we could have no photos of what we were seeing this magnificent night.

"Enough excitement for one night I think, let's head back." But then things got dicey. About 15 minutes later, on that pitch black trail except for Jaime's lantern, in front of us on the trail (still far from the normal, regular trail we had started out on), we saw faint lights, moving up and down, heard whispered talking, and the sound of horse hooves on the path, all coming toward us. A man at the front must have sensed us and called out, "Paren allí. No vengan más cerca o habrá líos" ["Stop right there. Don't come any closer or there will be problems"]. Jaime, not one to be threatened on his own "turf," said in a quiet voice, "Serás tú que debes cuidarte; aquí, la ley" ["You are the ones that should be worried; we are the Law"]. He whispered to us, "Stay in your tracks, get down to the side of the trail and above all, don't move, I'll have to investigate this." He moved ahead cautiously and was soon out of our sight. Then there was sudden shouting, a few swear words even I understood (but do not quote) and shots fired. Then all hell broke loose, the sound of a stampede of perhaps three or four horses ahead of us and the sound of footsteps of men fleeing the scene.

"Carajo, Amy, I think I peed my pants!" We lied on the ground, trying not to make a sound and a few minutes later a very sweaty, tired – looking Javier came back down the trail, with blood oozing out of one arm, carrying his Winchester in the other. Amy reacted first (she had first aid experience from the many AT trips, another of her on-call duties) and said in Spanish, "Give me your handkerchief, Mike, take off your belt and shirt, I'll tear it in strips to wrap that wound." Javier was evidently grateful for he did not resist. After a few minutes, taking a drink of water from our canteens and downing 4 aspirin Amy insisted upon, he gave us an abbreviated version of what just happened, all in Spanish which I am trying to remember and translate.

"Muchachos, this is a night to remember! Never had one quite like this." But he was smiling, although in pain. "I'm sure the horses and the men have gone on ahead, not wanting any more chances to be recognized or at worst, arrested. This is standard behavior for tomb robbers. We will head back to the lodge, but there is one sight in front of us I want to prepare you to see; it's not pretty, but perhaps you will understand the 'other side' of Tikal and its outlying ruins."

Up ahead there was a dead horse to the side of the trail, but all covered in blood, saliva oozing from its open mouth, and its eyes seemingly wide open. It was on its side, and still strapped to its back, a sort of wooden frame on each side, and ... holy shit ... what looked like parts of a Maya stela tied with rope on each side.

"Miguel y Amy, we were at the wrong place at the wrong time. This crew evidently had just robbed that stela from one of the outreaching sites and were making off with it. I shot at one or two of them, wounded one apparently, and the horse got in the way in the melee. Let's slowly and carefully go back to the Posada; I can't have you in danger." So, we walked for what seemed an hour, got to the Posada, and Javier ordered them to turn on the generator for light. Javier insisted he go to his headquarters nearby, report the incident, and get medical treatment there. "I'm sorry this turned out the way it did. I understand you leave mid-morning tomorrow. I'll try to get back here in the morning and fill you in. Oh, there is one thing I really want you do to tomorrow: get up at dawn, go in the site, climb to the top of Maler's Temple and just watch and listen. It will be icing on the cake for you."

We did just that, but with all that had happened plus the entomological crowd that night, little sleep took place.

We were in the main plaza at 6:00 a.m. What greeted us was fog, lots of it, the tall pyramids barely visible, but just as amazing, raucous noise we could not figure out at first, but then saw through the mist: a huge flock of multicolored macaws, all squawking as they flew. We watched, hugged each other, and agreed with Jaime, icing on the cake indeed! The noise stopped shortly and then there was silence. And this scene:

We climbed down from Maler's Temple, walked through the narrow walkway back to the main plaza and sat on the steps of the acropolis, full of wonder and grateful for the good fortune of seeing all this. By that time, we bade goodbye to the Temples, did the short walk back to the Posada, had breakfast, and packed our things. We had one hour before the bus call to the landing strip. Then, Javier Kax walked in, one arm heavily bandaged but smiling. He said, "This belongs to you (it was my belt). Sorry, but I don't think you want to see that shirt or pañuelo. I have to ask a favor: you did <u>not</u> see anything last night except for animals, verdad? Tikal does not need that kind of publicity and for sure your names do not need to be associated with me! They did not catch that group of whoever they were; you can melt into the Petén Forest very easily. I've seen it many times. But please, do not allow this to color your plans to come with your Travelers. I will just say they will not get last night's 'guided tour.'" Javier laughed, we joined him and thanked him profusely, mainly expressing a "Ten cuidado" ["Be careful!"]. He said duty called, bade his goodbyes, and we were left wondering if all had been an illusion or dream. (Shades of Calderón de la Barca's "La Vida Es Sueño"!) How would we ever top this? Amy said, "That was scarier than Chichén, Mike, and I think we literally dodged a bullet. I'll discuss all this over a drink or three back in the hotel in Guatemala City." Agreed.

There was one more scary moment, but maybe not the same. After getting way overheated in the sun on the airstrip, once again waiting to get on the airplane for "home," we finally boarded, waited for what seemed forever for the air conditioning to kick in. I held Amy's sweaty hand, but it turned cold and muggy as the pilot revved the engines to a fever pitch, released his wheel brakes, and we lurched to the end of the clay runway before barely clearing the trees. Heaving a huge sigh of relief, I asked the stewardess, "Can we get something strong to drink?" She laughed, saying it was not the first time Aviateca on the Tikal run got this request and gave us each two small bottles of Johnny Walker Red, glasses of ice and said, "Maybe then a very short nap before Guatemala City. I saw the ice, remembered Puerto San José but said the hell with it.

Back at the Hilton, drinks in the privacy of the lounge, we both got out respective notebooks, jotted down just an outline of what I have described these past few pages, promising to talk in depth, let it all settle in tomorrow. Amy said, "AT owes me one. Mike, I'm afraid it's back to the French restaurant." We reviewed all the events of the past three days, one by one, enjoyed dinner and collapsed into each other's arms that evening. It was good to be alive and, may I say, in love.

The next day was largely spent on work and planning; time was getting on. This is day 19 of the trip; we had planned on no more than 21 days or three weeks for us and for a possible AT trip. We contacted Nataniel and

# 12

## EXPLORING COPÁN

We were salivating at this final chance to see true Maya grandeur. Copán is in no way less important than Palenque, Uxmal or Chichén-Itzá in Mexico, or Tikal in Guatemala, in some ways more important. Someone called it the "Paris" of the Mayas. So, I'm spending some time to introduce it (all these travel blurbs would be used as a basis for the AT travel brochure, including many of the photos, that is, if it comes to fruition).

The Archeological Zone of Copán has been known since 1576! It is the "religious center" of one of the large Maya cities from the Classical Period which flourished from the 4th century A.D. The ruins are situated in the west part of the country of the Republic of Honduras and the capital of this Department is Santa Rosa de Copán. The town has 3000 inhabitants and is only an easy walk to the Ruins.

Of all the great cities founded by the Mayas, Copán was the first to be known, but we don't know exactly when and by whom. It is doubtful that the conquistadors arrived at this place. It was in 1576 when a member of the "Real Audiencia de Guatemala" described the site to King Felipe II in a letter. Three centuries passed before the next notice in 1834, and five years later the first expedition arrived at the site, that of John L. Stephens and Frederick Catherwood, the latter an artist from England, the former a North American Diplomat. The books of travel of the two, "Incidents of

Travel in Central America, Chiapas and the Yucatán" are yet today classics for both their commentary and inimitable lithographs.

The origin of the modern name "Copán" is discussed and debated, but it is attributed to an Indian chief called Copán-Calel who battled against the Spaniards in the 19th century.

The most famous modern scientist-discover of the site is Dr. Sylvanus G. Morley, author of many studies on the Maya, who made various trips to the site and in fact became a "citizen-resident" of the town, paying taxes, etc. It was he who wanted to restore the site and obtained funds to do so from the Carnegie Institute. (We've come across him before, i.e. the Mayas as "philosopher - priests," a misnomer and in his defense, not his fault – the hieroglyphs had not been deciphered!)

Copán is in a small valley formed by the Río Copán which flows north into the Río Motágua which in turn flows into the Atlantic. The principal agricultural products of the region are corn, beans and squash, not to mention the tobacco that came later. The latter came from Cuba, much of it planted since 1959 and the Fidel Castro regime when large tobacco farmers fled the island, but with seeds in hand! The soil is incredibly volcanic rich!

The oldest stela is from 465 A.D. and the last from 800 A.D. The site of Copán was known for its science and its arts, for the abstract astronomical calculation for the Maya Calendar (possibly, the Olmecs at Las Ventas in Mexico might argue with this), for its sculpture and its glyphs! A mouthful! The principal site consists in patios, stelae, small pyramids, temples, and the acropolis. It did not have the tall pyramids like Tikal. Never mind. The most significant works are indeed the stelae, the altars, the amazing ball court and the hieroglyphic stairway. (I am saying this academically, but Amy and I have now seen all the major Maya sites with the exception of tiny Bonampak with its worn frescos and a few others. We were dazzled by Copán in spite of no tall pyramids.)

The stelae and altars denote sixteen successive kings in the dynasty. Like Tikal, Calakmul, and other sites, Copán was governed by a royal king, with nobles, warriors, artisans, and slaves below him. One of its amazing stelae depicts the ascent to the throne of 18 Rabbit, his head coming out of the jaws of the earth monster, thus relating the king to the rising sun. (And perhaps the opposite, King Pacal entering the jaws at his death in Palenque).

Much more could or should be said: the classic city of Quiriguá, a rival of Copán is just 50 kilometers north, the place of the tallest stelae in all Maya country. One is 11 meters high, done in 771 A.D. A pity there was no time.

One added historical note: aside from the plethora of monuments to be seen, the archeologist Ricardo Gurcia discovered the amazing Temple of Rosalilla, unique in being perfectly preserved below a newer temple on top of it!

Now to the trip visit, and surprises.

When we headed east from Guatemala City a serious reminder of the 1976 quake reminded us of its severity: a major highway bridge taken out (our road was built on a makeshift bridge). We were told the roadbed had shifted a full three feet!

Wet and rainy, that was that day. We drove through many little towns and saw wonderful sights: a country church, thatched houses, local strange plants; Rodolfo knew them all.

We reached the Honduras Border and had a first inkling of inconvenience at best, the crossing of the border at a spot in the road and with a long wait on papers to get into Honduras – that traditional "rubber stamping" of the tourist cards (no reason we could figure out, we were the only car). Rodolfo was at first non-plussed, saying this was normal harassment and solved only by a generous "presente" to the cranky, slow-moving, and obstinate Honduran "customs official." Incidentally, before all this we waited an hour and a half for him presumably to finish "almuerzo" and we surmise a "siesta." The bribe taken, he rubber stamped the tourist cards, but said there was one more thing: all vehicles coming from Guatemala were possible carriers of some mysterious insect which could damage crops in Honduras. Ha. Was this real? Another fee. And then a hilarious fumigation of the van:

He did do us the courtesy of saying we could stand to the side, evidently not worried about any bugs we carried on our person (Amy laughed, wondering if any of those prize-winners from the Posada in Tikal might be in our pockets!) The guy, we named him "Happy Jack," had a smile on his face the whole time. Rodolfo said he probably was making horrendously low pay, thus the unofficial "fleecing" of tourists. Rodolfo said, "Enjoy it, just another small chapter of life in Latin America, right? Guatemala and Honduras are not on the best of terms anyway. It's complicated."

We did wonder if the reverse would be true getting back into Guatemala in just two or three days. Despite it all, we arrived in the town of Copán Ruinas (Santa Rosa de Copán) at about 4:00 p.m. Too late to go to the ruins, we did the Museum as an introduction. One photo suffices to show what we thought was its best artifact: the round carved stone which had been at the ball court (to come):

We were staying at the modest (understatement) Hotel Marina right off the town square, simple, but a big step up from the Posada de la Selva.

There seemed to be a fair number of young men and boys hanging out near the hotel; we would find out why later. The evening however was a good introduction to Honduras in several ways. While taking our ease on benches to the side of the Plaza, I saw a small "bodega" on the other side, investigated and found they were selling for a ridiculous price small Honduran cigars – 5 centavos for a small pack. We had to try them; there's a story.

It turns out a matter for an expert; I'm not; this tobacco is considered to be the finest of all Central America. When Fidel Castro took over Cuba in 1959 and a few months later declared himself to be an avowed Socialist, many rich landholders got out while they could. Some of them, growers of Cuba's famous tobacco (and makers of stogies) migrated to Honduras and the Copán Valley. The soil is volcanic, incredibly rich, and the locals say they actually "improved" on the Cuban product. Business expert Amy wondered if there were Rotarian Clubs in Honduras. Get it? Ha!

So we lit up; both of us had smoked cigarettes in younger days. After two or three of the tiny cigars we were both woozy and wondering if we would turn green. Discretion stopped the experiment at that point. But a pleasant turn of events followed that evening. I traded songs on the guitar that night in the tiny plaza, this while repeating cigars and beer with a young fellow from Tegucigalpa, working on a dig at the ruins. Sleep should have come easily after those beers, but we were awakened at about 4:30 a.m. with the clip clopping of horses' hooves on the cobblestone street outside. Then came firecrackers and voices singing. It turned out to be yet another procession (we had seen our share in Guatemala) with everyone carrying a candle and a group of men (the "cofradia" one supposes) carrying the image of our Lady of Perpetual Help. It all ended in the tiny church with a recitation of the Rosary. One could thank Our Lady for the lack of sleep. And an aside, we could have used her help to fix all the tires on the van. Those vagrants yesterday let out all the air of Rodolfo's tires. Fortunately, the hotel had a compressor.

We were excited to finally seen Copán Ruínas. Amy said it would be "icing on the cake" after all our travels (read: travails) and Guatemala. The first one sees is the "Jardín Paseo" to the ruins lined with many trees – the Árbol del Casamiento - with its many orange and yellow flowers. This place is reminding me more all the time of Santa Fé de Antioquia in Colombia of years back.

Then we entered the ruins proper and were dazzled by the Ceremonial Patio, really a quadrangular amphitheater. It is huge, and the stairs surrounding it were used (uh, probably) as seats in a stadium. We were told by guides that under each stela was a sort of deposit ["bóveda"] in which religious offerings were placed: vases, other ceramics, jade beads, and, hmm, bones.

We stopped to take this first scene all in, both of us really in awe. I remarked that the Hondurans have done an incredible job of "presentation" with immaculately kept grounds (we both wondered if they cut grass here as in Atitlán, with machetes!)

So the first and perhaps foremost artifacts of Copán were right in front of us – the stelae. The reader knows now about them, but one soon discovered why they call this place the "Paris of the Mayas." They are of stone carved in low relief with "portraits of kings" on two sides and the others bearing inscriptions with glyphs (it was in Copán that the amazing Linda Schele and her team who helped decipher the glyphs discovered the stelae were really historical markers, describing succeeding kings, queens and dynasties and "told the history of the Mayas.") In Copán they are monolithic, of a greenish stone called andesite, and are from 3 to 4 meters in height. It is believed they were done each 20 years (indeed, how long would it take?) or "katun" in Maya, probably corresponding to a human generation. "Of all that is Maya, things are always much more than they are perceived." The stelae certainly fit that statement; they are magnificent and awe-inspiring.

I remarked to Amy, "Those bastard tomb robbers in Tikal would need earth movers here, ha ha." Maybe not; there were reports of massive theft here in past years mainly due to the discover of those "deposits" I spoke of below each stela.

This first stela represents a masculine figure, looking straight ahead, with an advanced social standing: the figure displays sandals, a sort of stocking, large ear plugs, and a tall headdress with a mask of the sun at its apogee. The hands crossed in a seemingly pious way, carry a scepter of authority. The glyphs on the back side indicate a carving date of 731 A.D.! One can still notice traces of red pint which was the color on the stelae, a sacred color for the Maya.

Stela H is notable because it represents a feminine figure, the only one in Copán that represents a queen. She has a skirt of a Jaguar pelt to her knees and on top of the skirt, a sort of "over-skirt" with spheres, perhaps of jade, and ornate sandals. She sports a large sash about her waist and has a scepter in her hands. She wears large earrings or plugs, and a type of "helmet" or headdress covered with quetzal plumes. On the other side of the stelae there is a mask with the grotesque head of a bird; in the middle of the mask is the solar sun and at the base, glyphs. In the "bóveda" in front of the stela were found objects of jade and gold, the first time in such a closed monument. It is thought the precious stones came from Panamá or Colombia.

I can't talk now, but the question of the Quetzal Bird (the sacred bird of the Maya), I mean the real birds which are incredibly elusive but more incredibly beautiful, was discussed in the van on the way down here. More later. AT tradition of pursuit of nature is at stake here.

We have just today at Copán, so we have to keep moving. Amy and I spent much of the time reminiscing, both of us spending so much of our lives together at these places. We remarked, all things being equal and being in Latin America, someone is doing something right at all these sites, we surmise due to the true importance they have for Mexico, Guatemala, and Honduras. Generally, impeccably cared for! Something right, yes, notwithstanding outside interference at Palenque, Chichén and recently in Tikal.

It was next time to marvel at another monument at Copán, in my mind the most beautiful and best-preserved ball court in all Mesoamerica.

The Ball Court is to the south of the huge central plaza with its stelae. The court was in the form of a capital I, closed at the north end by steps and stelae and open at the south end. There were three markers on the sides: they took the form of three parrot heads, round, and symbols of the "day sun." More ritual than game, the ball game symbolized the forces of life versus those of death. Thus, it was not a sport as such, but with a religious character, and was only played by the noble class. It is believed it was played like the game in Mexico employed by the Aztecs and the Toltecs, but it in this case with each team of five players and a large hard rubber ball. One could hit the ball with any part of the body except the hands, and the ball may have weighed upwards to three kilos; therefore, the players wore special clothing or equipment to protect from the "blows." All this is suggested by literature and the spiel of guides; once again, "buyer beware." This however does not take away from the absolute beauty of the surroundings.

There is so much more to see and to tell, but as Jerry Reed would say (once again, in one of my favorite Country and Western songs, "We got a long way to go but a showat time to git theyah," in "East Bound and Down" for the film "Smokey and the Bandit," we got to keep movin!

One of the most mysterious, blabbed about, (maybe Adventurers would be as tired as I am now), monuments of all the Maya region is Altar Q (a replica at the Peabody Museum at Harvard). It is placed below the ballcourt and the hieroglyphic stairway (to come shortly). It is square with each side having four figures. The hat or headdress of each is distinct, and it is thought (aha!) the altar represents the 16 kings of the dynasty of Copán. Another idea, debated over the years, was that the 16 figures were "scientists or mathematicians" representing a sort of meeting where the Maya concept of 0 was established! This latter theory has been denigrated since the deciphering of the glyphs. Yet another "wild hair" (but not hairbrained) idea bandied about is that the figures are persons of authority, and that this altar was important in the history of the Mayas marking the computation of the year in 365 days. Amy and I said we would let them settle it.

Next to Altar Q is Copán's largest monument, what they call the Hieroglyphic Stairway, the "largest Maya inscription anywhere" according to site literature.

There are 63 steps or stairs, each with sculpted glyphs. There is a total of 2500 stone blocks. The problem is that the stairway was reconstructed by the anthropologists and archeologists after earthquakes which left the site severely damaged, and the "experts" had no idea which was the "proper order" of each stone, each with its own glyph. Work is still going on to try to straighten this out, and in a way it symbolizes much of what we call Maya Civilization and excavation at the same time, some 1200 years after its apogee.

In the center of the stairway are five statues of figures seated on luxurious thrones and one large altar. It is to note that in our time of 1980 only 30 blocks had been deciphered. Amy and I could only remember our time in Mexico a few years ago when we saw what the professors themselves called "the GOC pile," i.e. God Only Knows. Glad they had a sense of humor about it in that humidity and hot sun of the Yucatán. Scholars do know the stairway was constructed from 544 to 744 A.D., over a period of 200 years! It brings to mind bragging rights: we were told in scary Palenque (only for us, read the book) that the inscription in the temple at the top of the Temple of the Inscriptions was the largest "text" of the Mayas. Perhaps a matter of semantics.

The day was getting on, we were tired, thirst, sweaty and excited and amazed. There was much more we saw, much speculation, in the rain of Copán.

We were getting a bit zany by this time, and I suggested to Amy perhaps we should leave with a photo of the guy who was responsible for getting her here to meet a Maya end:

Rodolfo thought we should have a nice dinner in town (if one could be found), hopefully get a better night's sleep and have all day tomorrow for the drive back to Guatemala City. We were all thinking of Happy Jack at the border.

# 13

## AN UNLUCKY NUMBER BACK TO GUATEMALA

We were sure it would be a long wait, so that is why in part we did an early start. Rodolfo said you do not ever drive at night on this road! Be that as it may, it was just a short drive to the border, but about a half-mile before there were two army trucks and Honduran soldiers armed to the teeth. Speaking a Spanish far too fast for both Amy and me, an officer and Rodolfo entered into a spirited discussion. It turns out we would not have to worry about Happy Jack. Last night there was some kind of an encounter, a skirmish, hell I don't know, a gun fight at the border crossing. Happy Jack and an assistant were both found on the floor of his "office" bathed in blood and deceased to be sure.

The officer would not say much more except that the thieves, whoever they were, usually take roads little more than trails in the forests for their crossings, far from the "aduana" [customs]. They must have been confident they could pass inspection (another bribe!)! The soldier said he thinks it was tomb robbers since there have been other incidents near Copán recently. And I'm sure Happy Jack had cash and other "gifts" stashed in his office, maybe a simple robbery. Amy looked at me, her face pale in spite of that off and on sun yesterday and whispered, "Gaherty, this is issue number one for talk this evening at the hotel, that is, if we get to the hotel."

Much to our surprise, the soldier efficiently asked for our papers, approved, and waved us on through, but saying to stay on the main road to Guatemala City and not stop for any vehicles or people on the side of the road. Rodolfo smiled later, saying "I'll watch the speed limit (ha!) and get you folks home. Is AT research travel always this interesting? 'Ojo! Rateros en frente." ["Look out! Thieves ahead!"]. He laughed.

We reviewed the grandeur of Copán and Amy and I did agree it could not be matched or missed! This is when she brought up the Quetzal business. And I chimed in with diverse comments on Quetzal taxidermy. AT's reputation is for nature as priority, so the trips have such expert naturalists for the Adventurers. Guatemala certainly has the animals and we saw many of them, "But what about the birds? Toucans, parrots, parakeets, songbirds and most of all, the Quetzal (by the way I have not said but Guatemala's 'dollar' is called 'quetzal,' after the Maya heritage). The only one we have seen so far is a rather ratty looking stuffed bird in the museum of Guatemala at the beginning of the trip."

Rodolfo agreed that AT adventurers would insist on seeing the bird, but easier said than done. "They are near extinction, are rare, dwellers of dead pine forest in NE Guatemala, the area of Cobán. I have not suggested travel there because, aside from the remote possibility of seeing a Quetzal, the towns in the region were ravaged by the quake of 1976, and nothing matches what you have seen in Antigua, Atitlán or Chichicastenango. And you mentioned you have a time constraint."

I interjected, the professor once again: "I do recall that the famous defender of the Indians, Bartolomé de las Casas, served for years in Cobán. Oh well, he then served in Chiapas until the landowners ran him out and he died in Spain. We saw much about him in San Cristóbal de las Casas in Chiapas."

I then returned to reality and said, "Yes, the days have passed and frankly I've lost count, but it is now close to two- and one-half weeks. What say, Rodolfo, you do some research and let us know quetzal status and write to us back home. I personally think the ornithologists will be in high clover in Guatemala even without the quetzal. Amy?"

"Agreed for now, but the question is just tabled, not dismissed. We don't need to spend days on, pardon me, a 'wild goose hunt.'" Rodolfo had not heard that term and said he would recommend modifications of the same for Guatemala. There were no "Incidents of Travel in Guatemala" (borrowing a turn of phrase from the famous book by Stephens and Catherwood). No incidents thank God, and we pulled into Guatemala City at about 4 p.m. There was a closing visit with Nataniel of AT (Rodolfo called ahead), and over "cafecitos" we reviewed the trip. He was hopeful we could convince AT to proceed with our plan, assuring us that with care, planning and proper procedure (?), all would be a big success. Nataniel set us up with reservations for the Aviateca Flight to Los Angeles tomorrow morning; all bade goodbye and there was a bit of an emotional goodbye to Rodolfo at the hotel. "Cuidaste bien de nosotros!" ["You took good care of us."] He said, "Well, for the most part."

# EPILOGUE

After long, hot showers and fresh clothes Amy and I repaired to that familiar bar at the Hilton, had two drinks, and reviewed it all – Antigua, Puerto San José, el Lago de Atitlán, Chichicastenango, Tikal and lastly, Copán. The reader already knows the pros and cons, ups and downs, no point repeating now, but we both agreed to tell James Morrison at AT in Los Angeles all the details, leaving out nothing. We would just have to wait and see what he would say. It could go either way; our trip's events might even have boiled down to being either in the right or wrong place at the right or wrong time, something that can happen anytime, anywhere. Is that nebulous enough?

We were beginning to feel the alcohol, and maybe things got a bit maudlin. How long had it been? The first trip around Brazil on the International Adventurer where we met in 1973, the subsequent fun and adventure checking out Mexico for AT, and then the "old world" AT trip to Portugal and Spain in 1977, and now the Maya World. Wow! And we talked of the ups and downs of our own relationship. I pressed Amy for an answer, "Well, chica, where do we stand now?"

Amy laughed and said, "We are in a safe place in a beautiful country and maybe a little in love, enough to enjoy the 'restaurán francés' one last time." We did that, champagne, wonderful food (Mike was careful) and the best of all, making love afterwards in the room. As for the future, "mañana," after all, where are we?

# ABOUT THE AUTHOR

Mark Curran is a retired professor from Arizona State University where he worked from 1968 to 2011. He taught Spanish and Portuguese and their respective cultures. His research specialty was Brazil and its "popular literature in verse" or the "Literatura de Cordel," and he has published many articles in research reviews and now some fourteen books related to the "Cordel" in Brazil, the United States and Spain.

Other books done during retirement are of either an autobiographic nature – "The Farm" or "Coming of Age with the Jesuits" - or reflect classes taught at ASU on Luso-Brazilian Civilization, Latin American Civilization or Spanish Civilization. The latter are in the series "Stories I Told My Students:" books on Brazil, Colombia, Guatemala, Mexico, Portugal and Spain. "Letters from Brazil I, II, III and IV" is an experiment combining reporting and fiction. "A Professor Takes to the Sea I and II" is a chronicle of a retirement adventure with Lindblad Expeditions - National Geographic Explorer. "Rural Odyssey – Living Can Be Dangerous" is "The Farm" largely made fiction. "A Rural Odyssey II – Abilene – Digging Deeper" and "Rural Odyssey III Dreams Fulfilled and Back to Abilene" are a continuation of "Rural Odyssey." "Around Brazil on the 'International Traveler' – A Fictional Panegyric" tells of an expedition in better and happier times in Brazil, but now in fiction. The author presents a continued expedition in fiction "Pre – Columbian Mexico – Plans, Pitfalls and Perils." Yet another is "Portugal and Spain on the 'International Adventurer.'" "The Collection" is a summary of primary and secondary works on the "Literatura de Cordel" in Curran's collection. A return to academic research and work was "The Master of the 'Literatura de Cordel' - Leandro Gomes de Barros - A Bilingual Anthology of Selected Works." Now we present a return to the series of books dealing with research trips via Adventure Travel, a fictional account of "Adventure Travel" in Guatemala – Research of the Maya Heritage.

Published Books

A Literatura de Cordel. Brasil. 1973

Jorge Amado e a Literatura de Cordel. Brasil. 1981

A Presença de Rodolfo Coelho Cavalcante na Moderna Literatura de Cordel. Brasil. 1987

La Literatura de Cordel – Antología Bilingüe – Español y Portugués. España. 1990

Cuíca de Santo Amaro Poeta-Repórter da Bahia. Brasil. 1991

História do Brasil em Cordel. Brasil. 1998

Cuíca de Santo Amaro – Controvérsia no Cordel. Brasil. 2000

Brazil's Folk-Popular Poetry – "a Literatura de Cordel" – a Bilingual Anthology in English and Portuguese. USA. 2010

The Farm – Growing Up in Abilene, Kansas, in the 1940s and the 1950s. USA. 2010

Retrato do Brasil em Cordel. Brasil. 2011

Coming of Age with the Jesuits. USA. 2012

Peripécias de um Pesquisador "Gringo" no Brasil nos Anos 1960 ou □ Cata de Cordel" USA.   2012

Adventures of a 'Gringo' Researcher in Brazil in the 1960s or In Search of Cordel. USA. 2012

A Trip to Colombia – Highlights of Its Spanish Colonial Heritage. USA. 2013

Travel, Research and Teaching in Guatemala and Mexico – In Quest of the Pre-Columbian Heritage

Volume I – Guatemala. 2013

Volume II – Mexico. USA. 2013

A Portrait of Brazil in the Twentieth Century – The Universe of the "Literatura de Cordel." USA. 2013

Fifty Years of Research on Brazil – A Photographic Journey. USA. 2013

Relembrando - A Velha Literatura de Cordel e a Voz dos Poetas. USA. 2014

Aconteceu no Brasil – Crônicas de um Pesquisador Norte Americano no Brasil II, USA. 2015

It Happened in Brazil – Chronicles of a North American Researcher in Brazil II. USA, 2015

Diário de um Pesquisador Norte-Americano no Brasil III. USA, 2016

Diary of a North American Researcher in Brazil III. USA, 2016

Letters from Brazil. A Cultural-Historical Narrative Made Fiction. USA 2017.

A Professor Takes to the Sea – Learning the Ropes on the National Geographic Explorer.

Volume I, "Epic South America" 2013 USA, 2018.

Volume II, 2014 and "Atlantic Odyssey 108" 2016, USA, 2018

Letters from Brazil II – Research, Romance and Dark Days Ahead. USA, 2019.

A Rural Odyssey – Living Can Be Dangerous. USA, 2019.

Letters from Brazil III – From Glad Times to Sad Times. USA, 2019.

A Rural Odyssey II – Abilene – Digging Deeper. USA, 2020

Around Brazil on the "International Traveler" – A Fictional Panegyric, USA, 2020

Pre – Columbian Mexico – Plans Pitfalls and Perils, USA 2020

Portugal and Spain on the 'International Adventurer,' USA, 2021

Rural Odyssey III – Dreams Fulfilled and Back to Abilene, USA, 2021

The Collection. USA, 2021

Letters from Brazil IV. USA, 2021.

The Master of the "Literatura de Cordel" – Leandro Gomes de Barros, 2022

A Bilingual Anthology of Selected Works. USA, 2022

"Adventure Travel" in Guatemala – Research of the Maya Heritage. USA, 2022

Professor Curran lives in Mesa, Arizona, and spends part of the year in Colorado. He is married to Keah Runshang Curran, and they have one daughter Kathleen who lives in Albuquerque, New Mexico, married to teacher Courtney Hinman in 2018. Her documentary film "Greening the Revolution" was presented most recently in the Sonoma Film Festival in California, this after other festivals in Milan, Italy and New York City. Katie was named best female director in the Oaxaca Film Festival in Mexico.

The author's e-mail address is: profmark@asu.edu
His website address is: www.currancordelconnection.com

Printed in the United States
by Baker & Taylor Publisher Services